THE LIAHONA LEGACIES

Tunnels of Zarahemla

VOLUME III

A Novel by **TINA MONSON**

Acknowledgements

This book could not have been written without the support and assistance of a few very special people.

Carson, Carter, Sierra and Bristol, my wonderful children, they are the true inspirations behind the story. I'm grateful for their constant support, encouragement, and belief in me. Also, to Carson, for his help editing and to Carter, for helping with the illustrations.

A special heartfelt thanks to Suzette Jensen, my sister and editor, but mostly my friend. She is always available no matter the hour I need her. Her hard work and long hours on my behalf helped to quickly get the book to print. Thank you.

In addition, I would be ungrateful if I didn't extend a special thanks to Doyl Peck, his endless smile, positive attitude and large heart allowed me the ability to have computer problems, pass numerous deadlines, and place excessive stress on him. Thanks, Doyl for all your patience, but especially for being such a great friend.

Last, and most importantly, to my illustrator, husband, best friend, Kreg, without your love, and support, I would never have been able to complete this story.

Chapter One

Bear squealed from the sudden shock of cold that penetrated his entire body. Unexpectedly finding himself standing in chest-high water, he shivered uncontrollably. Confused at where he was and what had just happened, he looked with despair at Stick, Red and Runt standing next to him. Then he screamed in a scared voice, "What in the world happened? Where are we?"

Unsure of where they were, but certain they were no longer in the Treehouse, Stick swung his hand in the water, splashing Bear. "Be quiet, will ya?" he whispered.

Stick, nervous they might be in danger, cautiously scanned the area. With no one in sight, he maneuvered carefully through the fast-moving water toward the river-bank. Hoping they were somehow in the vicinity of Timber Creek, he scouted around the area for anything that might seem familiar. With one glance at the ancient-looking city approximately twenty yards away, Stick knew they were no where near the Treehouse, let alone the small town of Timber Creek.

Unsure where in *Book of Mormon* times they had traveled, Stick quickly lowered his body back into the cold water. Hoping that no one had noticed them, he motioned for his teammates to quickly do the same.

"Do you know where we are Stick?" Red asked soft-ly. He was nervous about Stick's actions.

"No! I have no clue. But if you want me to guess, I'd say we've traveled somewhere into *Book of Mormon* times," Stick replied. "I'm going to look around for a minute and see if I can get any indication of what time period in the *Book of Mormon* we've traveled to. Stay here. I'll be right back."

"I'm freezing, Stick!" said Bear. He held his mouth with his hand, trying to keep his teeth from chattering. "I can't stay in this water!"

"I'm cold too, Bear!" chattered Stick. "Hang in there for a minute, and I'll see if I can find somewhere safe for us to hide."

"Why isn't it safe to climb out here?" asked Bear.

"Bear, we don't want to get caught," replied Stick.

"Caught by who?" asked Bear.

"Caught by anyone," replied Stick. "We don't know where we are."

Fighting the strong current, Stick lifted his feet from the bottom of the river and allowed his body to be carried quickly down stream. Scouting out the area as he floated, he was unable to see anyone in the city.

"I wonder where everybody is?" he thought.

Dragging his feet along the bottom of the river to slow himself down, he drifted slowly past an opening that looked like a waterway into the city. Looking intently along the waterway, he noticed a series of red stones chiseled into the shape of blocks. They formed a wall that led toward the city in the distance.

The wall was approximately ten feet tall. It ran along the edge of the riverbank and ended at the edge of the city, where a twenty-foot tall, red brick wall surrounded the city. Stick struggled to see a series of buildings that were mostly hidden behind the large wall that surrounded the city. Determined to find out where they were, he focused on the buildings. He noticed several buildings, ranging from three to fifteen stories tall, with numerous symbols and designs that had been carved in the exterior of the building.

Stick turned his attention to the south part of the city, where he saw a dense forest filled with hundreds of birds sitting in the treetops. Stick loved birds and listened intently to the unique sounds they were making. He was positive that he could identify a few of them. As he studied the wilderness area, he was excited to see both a Coconut Palm tree and a Banana Palm tree.

"At least we won't starve," he thought to himself. Unable to see what the terrain was like to the north of the city, Stick dug his feet into the bottom of the river bed and stopped the current from pulling him down stream. He turned and started to walk against the current, back toward his teammates. As he looked down at the water, he was surprised to find it a bright emerald-blue color. The color was one he was sure he had never seen before. The water was almost transparent, and Stick could see the beautiful white sand usually hidden underneath the water. As Stick looked out across the river, he was shocked to see a bridge similar to the San Francisco Bay suspension bridge. It spanned the entire length of the river, about fifty yards, from shore to shore.

"How did I miss that?" he thought, shaking his head. "I must be cold."

Continuing his walk back toward his teammates, Stick noticed the sun setting in the west. He was amazed by the beautiful orange glow it cast through the clouds. As the light shined on the stones of the city it highlighted the designs etched on the buildings.

Bear, Runt and Red quietly waited for Stick to return. They listened to the peaceful sound of the water as it fell over the ledge next to the waterway, which supplied water to the great city. Suddenly, Runt noticed an army of men crossing the footbridge about five yards south of where they were standing.

Frightened, Runt squealed, "Look, Stick!" as he pointed to the oddly dressed men.

Stick held his finger to his mouth, signaling for Runt to be quiet. Then he quickly turned to see where Runt was pointing. Startled to see the men crossing the bridge, Stick quickly lowered himself into the cool water, hoping the men had not noticed him. The boys sat perfectly still, afraid to move, and watched until the men were almost off the bridge.

"Where are we, Stick?" asked Bear in a teary voice. "I want to go home to my mom."

"Ssshhh, Bear," replied Stick. "Follow me."

Stick slithered through the water like a snake, keeping only his head above the water. Red, Runt and Bear followed close behind. He cautiously guided the boys directly underneath the footbridge. He held his finger to his mouth again, reminding everyone to remain silent.

The boys watched as the army of men crossed the last few wood slats of the bridge. Red gasped in terror at their appearance. The men had both light and dark skin. They wore either a knee-length cloth wrapped around their waist or loose fitting pants. They had sashes tied around their waists and war paint on their legs, arms and faces. Most of them had long hair, dangly earrings, gold necklaces, and bracelets. Some of the bracelets started at their wrists and covered their arms all the way to their shoulders. All of the men had large, well-defined chests and legs. Each man carried a spear and one of the men even had a coyote head and fur draped over his head and shoulders.

Stick covered Red's mouth, nervous that the men above had heard him. He watched as two men with large, ornate headdresses stopped and looked over the side of the bridge.

"Keep moving men!" a deep, commanding voice shouted from the bridge.

Stick watched as the two men, slow to respond to the command, finally continued crossing the bridge.

Sure that the army of men was gone, Runt angrily asked, "What is the matter with you, Red? This isn't a joke! Depending on where we are in the *Book of Mormon*, we could be in serious danger if we're not careful."

"Yeah, Red. I don't want to get killed over one of your practical jokes!" added Bear, splashing water at Red's face.

"What are you talking about, Bear? It's your fault that we are here in the first place," shouted Red angrily, splashing water back in Bear's face.

"All right, you two. That's enough!" shouted Stick, quickly positioning himself between his two teammates. "We're already here, we just need to figure out how to get home—not fight with each other."

"You're right, Stick," groaned Red. "I know that, but I'm still angry. We wouldn't be here if Bear hadn't moved the Liahona."

"You wanted to see it too, if I remember correctly, Red," added Runt.

"I think we all wanted to see the Liahona," answered Red.

"Why are you still fighting?" asked Stick, frustrated by their behavior.

"Sorry, Stick," replied Red. "I'm just on edge. I don't like not knowing where we are."

"Neither do I, but you've got to stay in control of your emotions!" Stick replied.

"How do we figure out where we are?" asked Bear.

"That's a good question," replied Stick, deep in thought.

"We've got to get into the city and find someone to talk to that can give us an idea of where we are," said Runt.

"I agree," replied Red.

"Well, we can't walk up to the city dressed like we are and find out," said Bear, as he held up his grey t-shirt.

"The people in the city would know in a matter of seconds that we don't belong here," said Runt.

"I don't think it would take them more than a second to realize that we don't belong," replied Red. "But, I'm worried about the guards."

"So, then what's your idea?" snapped Runt.

"I don't have one, Runt. What's your idea?" Red shot back, annoyed by the question.

"You two fighting all the time isn't helping us!" Stick exclaimed angrily. "We don't need this childish fighting. We have enough to worry about."

"He's right, if we're going to figure out where we are you two have to get along," added Bear.

Red took a deep breath and let it out slowly. "Sorry, Stick," Red replied quietly.

"Yeah, Stick," said Runt. "I'm sorry, too. I'm just nervous."

"You should all know how this works. We have a limited amount of time to figure out where we are, what's wrong, and how to fix it," said Stick,

"No, I really don't know how all of this works," said Bear.

"Oh, yeah," replied Stick. "I forgot you weren't in the Treehouse when the Liahona unexpectedly took Hero, Bubba, KP and Bean on their adventure."

"So what has to happen, and what do I need to do?" questioned Bear.

"Well," Stick cautiously replied, "We're gonna have to find out where in *Book of Mormon* times we are, what has gone wrong, and then fix it as quickly as we can. And do it without getting hurt, caught, or killed."

"How long do we have?" asked Bear.

"We only have seven of the Lord's days here in this land, or we'll have to stay and live in this time forever," Red replied, not caring whether Bear was scared or not.

"Really? Forever?" Bear asked in a teary voice.

"Yep, forever!" replied Red.

"I don't want to stay here and freeze in the water forever!" cried Bear. "Stick, I wanna go home!"

"I guess you should've left the Liahona alone like Hero told you to do," snapped Stick, still frustrated and short tempered with the situation.

"How long are seven of the Lord's days?" asked Bear.

"I wish any of us knew," Red sharply answered.

"I'm sorry, Stick," said Bear, sniffing back tears. "I didn't want the Liahona to take us on an adventure. I just wanted to look at it for a minute. I didn't think adjusting it in the box would send us back to *Book of Mormon* times."

"The problem, Bear, is that we're not sure how the Liahona works," replied Stick. "That's why Hero told us not to play with it."

"Speaking of the Liahona, where is it?" asked Runt. "Don't we need it in order to get back home?"

"I don't have it," said Stick. "I don't know where it is."

The four boys looked at each other nervously for

several seconds before Red panicked. He ripped his backpack off his shoulders, and dragging it through the water made a splash that completely covered Bear. He pulled the zipper on the front pocket, checking for any sign of the Liahona. Panic covered his face as he looked up and said, "It's not in my backpack. I don't have the Liahona."

"I don't have it either," said Runt, looking up from his open backpack.

"Oh, this is great! No one knows where it is?" yelled Red, terrified by the silence.

"Relax a minute, Red," Stick said nervously. "I'm sure it's got to be close by. It's probably inside mine or Bear's backpack."

The boys, still shivering and cold, hid underneath the edge of the bridge, and watched as another guard crossed the wood planks above them, and slowly disappeared in the direction of the city. Red and Runt silently watched as Stick and Bear unzipped their backpacks and searched for the Liahona.

"It's right here! I've got it!" Bear exclaimed excitedly. He carefully held it up for everyone to see.

"Give that to me, Bear!" demanded Stick, reaching to take the Liahona from Bear's hands. "You've got to be careful! We need that to get home."

Bear held the Liahona just out of Stick's reach, taunting him as he said, "I can take good care of it. Besides it was in my backpack, I think that means I'm in charge of it."

"No, it doesn't mean that," said Red, reaching to take the Liahona from Bear.

"I'm sure you can take good care of it, Bear," replied Runt. "But Stick is the oldest, let him keep it safe for us."

Bear reluctantly held the Liahona up for Stick to take and then changed his mind. "No, I'm going to take care of it, Stick. I got us into this adventure or nightmare, whatever you want to call it, and I'm going to hold on to the Liahona until I can get us out of this mess."

"Bear, if you lose the Liahona, I'm not going to be happy," said Stick, nervous about leaving it with him.

"I will take good care of it. I understand how important the Liahona is," Bear replied, as he placed it inside the main pocket of his backpack. "Now zip up your backpack, I've got everything under control."

Stick looked at Bear, puckered his lips, and shook his head. Not wanting to take his eyes off Bear, he reached inside his backpack, searching for a piece of gum. Not finding it quickly, he looked down at the pack and shouted, "Hey, this isn't my backpack."

"Whose backpack is it then?" asked Red.

"This is Tater's backpack!" Stick replied nervously.

"Does it have any food inside?" asked Red. "I'm starving!"

"I'm sure it does, but everything inside here is soaked. We need to find a safe place to get out of the water," suggested Stick.

"Yeah, I'm freezing!" exclaimed Bear.

"Freezing? I'm now a prune, and I don't know how long it has been since I felt my feet," Runt complained.

"You're a prune? Look at my fingers," insisted Bear, holding up his hand for everyone to see.

Stick smiled as he looked around for a safe place to climb out of the water. Then he said, "Don't worry. I'm sure the Lord has a plan for us, we've just got to figure out what it is."

"Look at that!" said Runt pointing.

"What?" asked Stick, trying to see where Runt was pointing.

"There's a grate underneath the bridge, it could be a tunnel that leads to the city," he replied.

"What if instead of getting out of the water in the open, we follow the water under the bridge to the city and stay protected inside this?" asked Runt.

"Is there an entrance to the tunnel?" asked Bear.

"Yeah, look. This grate covers the opening to the city, but there is a small opening just under the water," replied Runt.

"How can you tell?" asked Stick.

"The water is practically clear," replied Red. "I can see the opening, too."

Stick took one last look around the area, checked out the opening in the grate and said, "That's a great idea, guys! We could make it all the way inside the city under the cover of the tunnel. I think at the very least we'd be safe."

"We don't have any idea what's really behind the grate, so, who wants to go first?" asked Runt sarcastically.

"I will," replied Bear. "I don't care what's behind the grate, as long as I can get out of this cold water soon."

"Wait, Bear. Let Red go first—just in case there's anything or anyone on the other side," suggested Stick.

"I have to go first?" Red asked tentatively.

"Come on, Red. Quit whining! We need someone a little older to lead the way," insisted Stick. "Can you handle it, or does Runt need to go first?"

"I can do it, thanks!" Red replied, as he took a deep breath and disappeared underneath the water.

Chapter Two

He ro sat motionless, holding his head in his hands. Nearly five minutes passed before he looked up at Bubba and said, "I'm not sure how we're gonna be able to cover for those four being gone very long. We've got some major damage control to do."

"What would you like me to do first?" Bubba asked, walking over to the table and putting his hand on Hero's shoulder, trying to console his brother.

"How can I help?" Squeaks shouted in a cheery voice.

"I'm here to help, too," offered Tater.

"So, what do you want us to do?" chimed in Butch. "I'm willing to help, also."

"The first thing we need to do is to make sure we have a set of scriptures up here. Then we'll be ready to help them with the information they need to get home if they call us on the walkie-talkie for help," answered Hero.

"Good idea," said Butch.

"They know about the walkie-talkies, don't they, Tater?" quizzed Hero.

"Do they even have a walkie-talkie with them?" Bubba asked tentatively.

"Oh man, I hadn't even thought about that!" replied Hero. "What are they going to do?"

"Before we all freak out, where are all of the walkie-talkies?" asked Bubba.

"I don't have one," said Squeaks.

"You have one in your backpack, Hero," said Bubba. "You have the one we just brought back from our *Book of Mormon* adventure."

"Tater, you had the one from the house," said Butch. "Is it still in your backpack?"

"Where is my backpack?" asked Tater, looking around the Treehouse. "I thought I left it over there in the corner," he said as he pointed.

"I'm sure it's in here somewhere," said Squeaks. "I'll help you look."

Everyone quickly searched the room. Butch even checked the balcony to see if Tater had left it outside. But the backpack was nowhere to be found.

"It's not in the Treehouse, Tater," said Bubba. "Are you sure you didn't take it to the house?"

"I'm positive I didn't take it to the house. In fact, I know for certain I left it here in the Treehouse," Tater responded, frustrated he could not find his pack. "I had it right next to me, so if you called, I could answer the walkie-talkie really quick."

"Didn't Stick come up here to get your backpack, Tater?" asked Squeaks. "I thought that was why the boys came up here."

"Yeah, that's right! Mom wanted her walkie-talkie back, remember?" Bubba asked excitedly.

"Do you think Stick took the backpack with him?" asked Squeaks.

"Oh, I hope so," replied Tater. "The walkie-talkie was in there, along with my scriptures and some food. They would at least have a few things to help them."

"That's one good thing about this mess," said Hero, biting his lip nervously.

"Let's get ready in case they call. Do we have scriptures up here?" asked Bubba, shuffling through the books on the table.

"Mine are here!" Butch yelled, as he unzipped his backpack and quickly searched through its contents. Unable to find them, he looked up at Hero and said, "Well, I thought I had my scriptures."

"I have mine," said Squeaks, patting the side of her backpack.

"Well, will ya get them for me, sis?" asked Bubba, grinning at her excitement.

Squeaks set her backpack on the floor, unzipped the

pocket and retrieved a small, blue triple combination. She proudly held up the book with a smile that covered her entire face and said, "Here they are, Bubba!"

"Good job, Squeaks," he replied, taking the scriptures from her hand. "By the way, while I was gone, I sure missed seeing your pretty smile."

"I missed you too, Bubba," said Squeaks, sporting a big, cheesy grin.

"Hey, Tater, will you help Squeaks clear off the table and set the scriptures up there?" asked Bubba. "Hero, why don't you grab your backpack really quick and get the walkie-talkie, we're gonna need to make sure the batteries are charged for when the guys try to contact us."

Hero agreed and quickly found his backpack. He retrieved the walkie-talkie and placed it on the table. Then he nervously looked up and asked, "Tater, did you have fresh batteries in the walkie-talkie?"

Tater thought quietly for a moment before he responded, "You know, I'm not sure, but I think I had a fresh set in my backpack."

"Let's hope that you did," said Hero, crossing his fingers and holding them up for everyone to see.

"What do we do now?" asked Squeaks. "What else can I do to help?"

"Nothing right now, Squeaks. We just need to wait," answered Hero. "There's not much else we can do."

"I had to do that while you were gone," Squeaks replied disappointedly. "And it wasn't very easy. All I did was worry."

"And that's all we're going to do this time," said Hero. "Worry!"

"That, and try to cover for those four. Tater, do you know if they had anything worked out with their parents?" asked Bubba.

"I think Bear checked with his mom, and she said it was okay for him to stay over and play for a couple of days," said Squeaks. "So, I think he's okay."

"Red's mom was okay with whatever," added Tater. "But Stick's mom wanted him to check in sometime today. I think he was supposed to mow and edge his and his grandma's yards today."

"What about Runt? Does anyone know anything about him?" asked Hero.

"I'm not sure about Runt," replied Tater. "I don't remember what he was supposed to do."

"I know what he was gonna do," Butch said in a soft voice.

"What? Tell us," insisted Hero.

"Runt was going to come over to my house today. His mom and dad are out of town for the weekend, and he is staying with my family," Butch answered sadly.

"What's the matter, Butch?" asked Squeaks. "Are you okay?"

Butch looked at Squeaks, took a deep breath and slowly blew it out before he finally answered. "I'm the only one who hasn't gone on a *Book of Mormon* adventure yet," he responded sadly.

"Wait a minute, Butch," insisted Tater. "Neither have I, remember?"

"Me neither!" added Squeaks. "I haven't been on an adventure yet either!"

"Yet?" squawked Hero. "If I have my way, no one will go on another adventure! At least not until we're older and don't have to worry about getting into trouble. This adventure stuff is a little too nerve racking."

"I want to go once before I'm older. I've always wondered about Captain Moroni and the two thousand stripling warriors. I'd love to meet some of them. Or meet Christ when He came to visit the people. That would be so amazing," insisted Butch. "I can think of a lot of great times in the *Book of Mormon* that I'd like to visit."

"The problem, Butch," interrupted Bubba, "is that you don't get to choose where or when you go in the *Book of Mormon*. You could just as easily end up in the middle of a war, or worse."

"Worse—what could be worse than war?" asked Squeaks.

"Well, think about the *Book of Mormon*, Squeaks," said Bubba. "You could end up in the middle of the terror of the Gadianton robbers, or be put in jail during King Noah's time. I can think of a lot of things that are worse than war."

"I don't want to end up in any bad stuff," Squeaks replied anxiously. "But I still want a chance to go back to *Book of Mormon* times."

"Well maybe sometime after Stick, Runt, Red and Bear get back from wherever they are, we'll get our turn to go," Tater suggested excitedly.

"Only, when we go, we'll be prepared," teased Squeaks.

"Yeah," agreed Bubba. "Going on our adventure might have been a lot less stressful if we had gone with everything we needed."

"Like what?" asked Squeaks.

"Like clothes!" answered Bubba. "The right kind of clothes would have been really helpful."

"Don't worry guys. When the Liahona needs us to fix something in the *Book of Mormon* again, we'll be totally prepared with clothes, food, medicine—everything we could possibly need," said Hero.

"That's if we get the guys home," added Butch, trying to be realistic. "I guess there won't be any more adventures if we don't get them and the Liahona back."

"We'll get them back. And when we do, I'm gonna ring Bear's little neck for taking the Liahona out of its box," declared Bubba.

"How do you know Bear took the Liahona out?" asked Squeaks.

"Oh, come on, Squeaks!" replied Bubba, rolling his eyes. "This is Bear were taking about. You know it was his idea to take it out of the box. He probably talked Stick into taking the box out of the trophy case just because he wanted a closer look at it!"

"I can see him talking Stick into that," she replied, nodding in agreement.

"I sure wish they'd left the box alone," Hero said sadly. "They could be in so much trouble right now."

"Don't worry, Hero. They're strong guys," said Butch, trying to be positive. "I'm sure they can handle wherever they are."

"Are we talking about the same people, Butch?" asked Bubba, grinning.

"Have you ever seen how Stick handles bugs? Snakes? Bats? Anything creepy, crawly or slimy?" exclaimed Bubba. "He turns into a basket case. He can't handle them at all."

"Do you remember when we were in the bat tunnel with Lehonti?" asked Butch, laughing. "Stick was flippin' out. He thought tip-toeing would help us all."

"How about when he ran into the snake climbing down the cliffs?" asked Bubba, snickering. "He handled that really well."

"Well? All I can remember is him running around, screaming and waving his hands wildly, almost knocking several of us to the bottom of the cliffs," said Tater, shaking his head at the memory.

"Or how about Red? I'm not sure he can be serious for more than a minute. What happens when he tries to pull a prank on someone back there?" Squeaks asked.

"That ought to go over well," Bubba remarked sarcastically.

"Or Runt—what about him? He likes to play pranks, too," added Hero. "What's going to happen when they're not serious at a time that they need to be?"

"Pranks? I think Red just tries to see what he can get away with," said Bubba. "Hopefully, he'll be able to see that *Book of Mormon* times might not be the best time to mess around."

"What happens if he doesn't and he pulls some dumb prank?" asked Butch.

"Well, depending on where they have gone, pranks may get them killed," replied Bubba.

"Killed?" Squeaks asked in a terrified voice.

"Oh, probably not killed. But he could get into a lot of trouble," said Hero.

"I think Stick may be the only one who can be serious for more than a minute," said Butch, smiling.

"I miss them already," Squeaks said sadly. "Do you think they are going to be okay?"

"They're going to be just fine," answered Bubba, reassuring Squeaks. "Stick may not like bugs, but when it comes to *Book of Mormon* knowledge, he knows more than anybody I know."

"I agree, Squeaks. They're going be just fine. I know that they're gonna be able to figure out what they need to do and be home before you know it," added Hero. "I wonder if they'll get to meet prophets and people they've read all about in the *Book of Mormon*. I bet they're making some great friends right now."

"Kinda like we did on our adventure," added Bubba. "People like Captain Lehi, Captain Moroni and even Comonti. They turned out to be great friends. In fact, I miss them all already."

"I sure hope our teammates ended up in a peaceful time in the *Book of Mormon*," Squeaks said hopefully.

Chapter Three

Stick was the last one to squeeze and wiggle his way into the city's water system. Once he was inside, the four boys headed east through the water, toward what they hoped was a place to enter the city.

"I wonder exactly where we are," said Red, as he struggled through the waist-high water.

"I'll bet we're somewhere in *Book of Mormon* times," Runt replied, through a cheesy grin.

"Oh really? Do you think so?" Red asked sarcastically, as he splashed water at Runt.

"Yep! I'm pretty sure," replied Runt, holding up his hand to block the water.

"I'm glad you two still have a sense of humor," snorted Bear. "'Cause... I sure don't. I'd like to go home. I'm not sure I want to be here."

"Come on, Bear. We can either have a positive attitude, or we can feel sorry for ourselves. I'm afraid if we do that we're gonna end up stuck here somewhere in *Book of Mormon* times forever," insisted Stick.

"Forever?" shrieked Bear. "What do you mean, forever?"

"Remember, we only have a week of the Lord's time to solve what has gone wrong and correct it, or we'll be stuck here forever," answered Runt.

"Is that how it worked when Hero and Bubba were on their adventure?" Bear asked nervously.

"Yes, Bear. Didn't you pay attention?" snapped Red.

"Yeah, I paid attention. Red," Bear replied defensively. "I just forgot."

"Hey, look. The water level isn't quite as high here," said Red. "It's only as high as my thighs now."

"The water is still as high as my chest, Red!" Bear complained. "And it's really hard to walk. I don't think I can do this anymore."

"You can do it, Bear," encouraged Stick. "We've got to be getting close to the city by now. Hang in there."

"I need a raft, canoe, something I can sit on for a while. Even paddling would be a lot easier than walking," Bear whined exhaustedly.

"I wish we had a canoe. That would be great! It would make moving through this water a lot easier," said Red. "Good idea, Bear."

"Where could we find one?" asked Runt. "My legs are tired, too."

"Well, we're not going to find anything down here," answered Stick. "These tunnels have to be part of the city's water system. I bet this water is what they drink, bathe in and use for their crops. There's not much chance of finding anything to float on in this water."

"Hey, look!" yelled Bear. "There's a log up ahead! Maybe we could use it for a raft," he suggested excitedly. He ran toward the floating wood, straining every muscle in his body to push quickly through the water.

"WAIT!" screamed Stick.

Surprised by the sudden scream, Bear stopped abruptly and turned around to look at Stick. "What's up, Stick?" asked Bear. "You scared me!"

"That's not a log! That's a crocodile!" Stick hollered. "Everybody, get out of the water, quick!"

"Where? Where do you want us to go?" Red asked frantically, turning in circles as he tried to locate a place to climb out.

"There isn't any place to climb out here!" yelled Bear. "What should I do?"

"Crocodiles? There aren't any crocodiles in South America," Runt calmly reasoned. "That can't be a crocodile."

Bear breathed a sigh of relief at Runt's comment, remembering that Runt was an expert on reptiles and animals.

"Alligators and caimans live in South America, but not crocodiles," insisted Runt.

"What? Are you sure?" Bear asked in a squeaky voice. "That could be an alligator?"

"Yeah, I'm sure," replied Runt. "That log is most likely an alligator."

As Runt finished his sentence, Bear started screaming. "What should I do? What should I do?"

"Just hold still, Bear. Maybe it will float on by," suggested Stick.

"It's not going to float by!" Red yelled angrily. "Alligators don't float past food."

"Food?" whimpered Bear, afraid to move a muscle. "Stick, please help me! I don't want to be alligator food."

Runt, suspicious of the slow moving gator, cautiously moved toward Bear. He watched quietly as it came to the surface for a few seconds, then submersed itself for several seconds, repeating this process over and over as it headed toward the group.

"Hold really still, Bear," whispered Runt. "And you, too, Red. It's close."

Bear, positive he was about to be dinner for the alligator, closed his eyes, folded his arms across his chest and tried to anticipate where the alligator would attack him first.

Runt continued to watch as the large reptile submersed itself one last time, about three feet from Bear's body. Disappearing underneath the water for several seconds, it gave no sign of where it might be.

Suddenly, Bear screamed at the top of his lungs, startling the boys. "My leg! My leg! He's on my leg."

Runt, sure Bear was being attacked, rushed to his aid. Splashing through the water loudly, hoping to distract or scare the alligator from biting Bear.

"Where's it biting you, Bear?" Runt yelled, as he continued to swing wildly in the water.

"It's not biting me," Bear answered, still screaming. "It's rubbing its slimy scales on my leg. I hate slimy things," Bear replied, as he hopped around, trying to rub the slimy feeling off his legs.

"It's not biting you?" asked Runt as he wiped water from his face. "Then where is it?"

"Aaaaaahhhhhhh!" Stick suddenly screamed. "Aaaaahhhhhh! It's touching me! It's touching me!"

Runt turned and raced to Stick's aid, hoping his splashing and yelling would chase away the alligator. "Is it still touching you?" yelled Runt, as he continued running.

"Yes, it's touching me. I think it's wrapping itself around my legs," Stick cried nervously. "Runt, get it off! Get it off!"

Runt, unable to see the reptile from above the water, dove beneath the water to get a better idea of what was after them. He was suddenly face to face with a jagged-toothed eel, which was trying to wrap itself around Stick's flailing legs.

Runt grabbed the eel's tail and pulled with all his might. The eel tightened his grip on Stick's legs and Runt was unable to pull it free. In need of air, Runt stood up, took a big gulp of air and quickly dove back underneath the water. Taking hold of the eel's long, gray, slimy tail, he forcefully pulled and twisted until he removed it from Stick's legs. Then watched as the six-foot-long eel quickly swam toward the river.

Runt stood up, gulped another breath of air and wiped the water from his face and eyes.

"Did you get it?" asked Red, nervously searching for the eel. "Is the alligator still here somewhere in the water?"

Runt smiled, coughed a few times and then replied, "That wasn't as alligator, guys. That was an eel."

"Did you get it? Or is it coming after me next?" Red asked nervously, still frantically searching the area.

"No, it's not coming after you. It headed toward the opening into the river. I think you're safe," Runt answered with a smile.

"Is it going to come back?" Bear asked apprehensively. "That was the grossest feeling I've ever felt on my legs before."

"I don't think so. It swam away pretty fast," replied Runt. "You big chickens. I was the one who had to grab a hold of its tail."

"I'm not chicken!" protested Stick. "That thing had my feet tied up, and I couldn't get any leverage to fight it."

"Yeah right, Stick," teased Red. "Even you know you're afraid of bugs."

"You screamed the entire time Runt was under the water, Stick," added Bear. "You know you were afraid."

"Of bugs and snakes maybe, but not fish," Stick snarled angrily.

"What do you think eel's are, Stick?" asked Runt.

"They're water snakes," interrupted Bear. "They even have big teeth."

"That's right, Bear," agreed Runt. "And I saw it up close."

"Well, whatever it was, I wasn't afraid of it," argued Stick.

"Guys, I've had it with the water. Instead of you three arguing, can we just find a place to climb out of here?" interrupted Red, as he tried to smooth the wrinkles out of his hands.

"Yeah, let's get rolling!" agreed Bear. "I'm water logged, too."

"Do you think we'll be safe?" Stick asked nervously.

"Probably safer than staying here," said Runt. "That eel could come back."

"Or there could be more ahead," replied Stick.

"I guess there's only one way to find out," answered Runt, as he started moving through the water and further into the tunnel.

Red hurried to stay up with Runt, not wanting to get too far behind. They were followed closely by Bear and Stick. They had twisted back and forth through several hundred yards of tunnels when Bear noticed hieroglyphics all over the walls.

"Hey, guys, look at the hieroglyphics on the wall," Bear said as he pointed. "What do you think they are?"

"Writings of some kind," answered Stick.

"Writings for who? And why would someone have etched all these pictures and symbols down here?" Runt asked, obviously confused. "No one's ever going to see them."

"I'm sure it was either the Lamanites or Nephites that made them," Red replied matter-of-factly.

"Wow, you are so smart, Red!" Runt said, sarcastically, shaking his head.

"Will you two focus for a minute?" Stick asked angrily. "This situation is not a joke."

"Sorry, Stick," replied Runt. "Joking is how I deal with stress."

"What do you think all these writings mean?" asked Bear, as he walked closer to the wall and rubbed his finger across the stones.

"Maybe someone likes to chisel," said Runt, nodding his head and trying to act serious.

"That, or do you think this could be a secret message?" Bear asked excitedly.

"Well, I doubt anyone would chisel a secret message into the stone down here. But the pictures are really cool," said Stick, looking closely at the hieroglyphics.

"Why wouldn't someone send a secret message this way?" asked Bear, annoyed by Stick's response.

"Think about it, Bear," replied Red. "The message wouldn't be kept secret for very long, would it?"

As Stick, Red and Runt laughed and teased Bear, a tear trickled down his face. He was overwhelmed by the stressful situation the four boys were facing.

"Come on, Bear. We didn't mean to hurt your feelings," said Stick. "We're just teasing."

"Hey, everybody quiet! Did you hear that?" Bear asked softly.

"Hear what, Bear?" questioned Stick.

"Voices—I heard voices," he whispered.

"I don't hear anything," replied Red, as he continued to splash around in the water.

"Me neither, Bear. I don't hear anything," said Runt.

"Be quiet and listen then," said Bear, annoyed by Red and Runt's teasing.

"Be quiet, you guys," insisted Stick. "I thought I heard something, too."

"What is it?" asked Red, continuing further down the tunnel.

"Sssssshhhh," whispered Stick, as he grabbed Red's arm and pulled him back. "We don't know who's up there."

"Come on, you guys. Quit being so paranoid!" replied Red. "It's not like whoever it is—is going to come after us. They might be able to help us."

"I'm the oldest, so I'm in charge! Now come back here and be quiet," Stick demanded, as his face turned bright red.

Red quickly moved behind Stick and said, "Sorry, Stick. I was just playing around. I didn't mean to make you mad."

"I know. But quite frankly, Red, I'm sick of the jokes. Let's try to find out where we are and what we need to do to get home without getting killed, okay?" replied Stick, in a low, gruff voice.

Red, not wanting to cause any further problems, nodded. The boys then quietly followed Stick deeper through the underground water system, toward the city and the mysterious voices. They walked for nearly ten minutes and had traveled only an additional fifty yards through twisting tunnels of waist-high water. Then Runt noticed, as he looked over his shoulder, that he had no idea where they had come from or how to get back out to the river.

"How far have we traveled?" asked Runt. "The city didn't look like it was this far, did it?"

"Yeah, how far have we traveled?" asked Red.

"And how are we ever gonna find our way back outta here?" asked Bear. "I think these tunnels go on forever."

"I was just thinking the same thing," said Runt. "I'm starting to get a little nervous. Maybe there is no end to these tunnels."

"Don't get nervous," whispered Stick. "I think we've probably traveled close to a half mile. I'm sure we can still find our way back out."

"Yeah, but the city wasn't a half mile away from the river we were standing in, was it?" asked Bear.

"No, but we've wandered back and forth through these tunnels at least that far," replied Red.

"Sewer and water systems never run in a straight line, you guys," reasoned Stick. "I'm sure we're close."

"Close to what?" asked Bear, obviously frightened by his surroundings.

"Close to those guys," replied Runt. He pointed to a small platform fifty feet further into the tunnel, where several men in black robes were standing. "Sssshhhh. They don't look like men who would be very willing to help us."

The boys quickly moved back into the safety of the tunnel and hid around the corner, hoping the group of men had not seen them. Stick slowly peered around the corner and counted five men. Squinting his eyes tightly, he tried to focus on the face of the man talking, but he was unable to see any distinguishing features. In fact, he could not see any of the men's features because of the dark clothes and robes covering their bodies.

"Who are they?" whispered Bear.

"I can't tell," Stick answered quietly.

"Do they look friendly?" asked Red.

"I don't think so," answered Stick.

"Can you hear what they're saying?" asked Bear.

Suddenly, one of the men looked up toward Stick. Stick quickly pulled his head back around the corner, not wanting to be seen. He quickly placed one finger across his lips, motioning for Bear to be quiet. Several tense seconds passed before Stick stuck his head around the corner again, hoping to hear what the men were saying.

"Captain Gilead has ordered the death of Nephi," said the tallest man.

"How does he want him killed, Giddianhi?" asked another man.

"We have learned that Nephi is to enter the city sometime in the next few days. Kidnapping the prophet has worked. Nephi is returning to save him, just as we planned. While he is searching, we will have opportunities to kill him," Giddianhi replied boldly.

"There are many men who travel with Nephi," replied another man. "How will we get close enough to kill him without being seen?"

"Your job, right now, is not to kill him, but to follow him around the city. Make sure you are not seen. As you follow him, stay hidden, and report where he goes and to whom he speaks. We will then know if anyone in the city of Zarahemla is disloyal to Captain Gilead," said Giddianhi.

"Wouldn't it be better for us to sway Nephi into serving Gilead with us, Giddianhi?" asked another man.

"That can't be done. Once we know who does not support us, we must kill Nephi," insisted Giddianhi. "More power and riches will be ours if he is dead."

"He could sway many to serve with Gilead's army," suggested a younger man.

"That is not the plan at this time. Many will follow us without him," insisted Giddianhi. "The desire of men's hearts is gold. With Gilead and Gadianton's men, they will have that."

"What, then, is our secret plan?" asked the younger man.

"Gilead requests you sharpen your blades. In three nights, we will meet again and Gilead himself will reveal to us how we are to kill the ex-Chief Judge, Nephi," Giddianhi explained.

"Where and when do we meet?" asked the young man.

"We will meet in this very place at noon day, and the Chief Judge will be dead before sunset," Giddianhi replied, smiling.

"Giddianhi," interrupted one of the men, "someone is watching us."

All five men turned quickly and stared into the darkness. Stick stood absolutely still, hoping no one could see him.

Suddenly, the eel brushed up against Bear's leg. He jumped up, trying to get away from the slimy feeling, and accidentally made a loud splash.

"Go men! Go find the spy!" yelled Giddianhi. "No one can know of our plan."

"Oh boy, we've got trouble! Come on, guys. We gotta go," yelled Stick. "They heard us!"

"Where are we going?" asked Bear.

"Just follow me, quick!" ordered Stick. He turned and started to move toward a small platform twenty feet in the distance. "Look! There's a staircase up ahead. Maybe it will get us out of the waterway and into the city."

"What if it doesn't?" asked Bear, trying to keep up with the others.

"Well, then we're gonna be killed!" screamed Red, struggling to move through the water. "'Cause they're right behind us now! So, move it or lose it, Bear!"

The boys struggled through the waist-high water to get to the platform. With every step, they could hear the men closing the distance between them, yelling for them to stop or be killed.

Chapter Four

Runt threw his backpack onto the platform and slowly pulled himself out of the water. His legs ached from the cold water that they had been stuck in for the last few hours. As he struggled for the strength to stand, he could see the men only a few yards behind. Then he noticed Bear scrambling to get his leg onto the platform. Instinctively, he reached down and grabbed hold of Bear's arm, pulling him from the waterway. Red and Stick tried to hurry, but seemed to move in slow motion as they maneuvered their way out of the water.

With everyone finally free from the cold waterway, Stick screamed, "Keep your fingers crossed that the door at the top of these stairs opens into the city." He turned and started running up the stairs as fast as his weak, water-logged, legs would carry him.

Red, struggling to get his legs to hold his weight, moved slowly as he followed the other boys. He was already several feet behind. He reached down, picked up his backpack and threw it over his shoulder. As he turned to climb the stairs, one of the evil men reached the platform. He grabbed hold of Red's leg and snarled, "I'm going to kill you, boy."

Red frantically called, "Help! Help me!" He shook his leg, desperately trying to free it from the man's grip.

"They can't help you, boy. No one can help you," he roared.

The man kept a tight grip on Red as he pulled himself out of the water, then reached into his cloak and retrieved a small dagger. Stick, Runt and Bear watched helplessly as their teammate's life was threatened. Red was horrified as the man lifted the dagger above his head and took aim at Red's chest.

Adrenalin took over Red's body, frantically he shook his leg and pulled himself free of the man's grip. Finding the strength to jump to his feet quickly, Red grabbed his backpack and swung it across the entire length of the platform, knocking three of the men back into the water. He frantically raced up the thirty or so stairs toward his friends.

Runt grabbed the big, castle-like door and pulled.

"I can't get it! Help me!" yelled Runt, as he heard splashes and yells from the men at the bottom of the stairs.

Suddenly full of strength, Red took hold of the door and pulled. With the two boys pulling, the door finally started to creak. Excited to see it move, Stick grabbed hold of the door and helped his teammates. As the screams from the men grew closer, Red pulled one last time. Groaning loudly, the door finally gave way enough that the boys could escape into the darkness of the city.

"Help me, quick!" yelled Red, once they were all outside. "Hurry, pull the door closed."

"That's not going to stop them, Red," said Bear, wanting to run and hide.

"I know that, Bear. I was hoping to slow them down," replied Red, pointing down the staircase.

Bear quickly stuck his head into the opening to see where the men were. Red, annoyed, took Bear's arm and pulled him from the opening, just in time to slam the door on the men inside.

"Where to?" asked Stick, unsure where they should go.

"Anywhere," answered Red, pulling Bear's shirt. "Just run!"

Although the moon was bright, the boys could not see anything in their path. They struggled through the city, weaving in and out of alleys, behind buildings and across cobblestone roads. Stick ran most of the time with his head turned, looking over his shoulder, unsure if the men were still following.

"Can you see anyone, Stick?" called Runt.

"Not right now," he replied, squinting as he stared into the darkness.

"Do you think we've lost them?" asked Bear, completely out of breath.

"I'm not sure," responded Stick.

"Well, if we can't see them at all, do you think we're safe?" quizzed Bear, wanting to stop running.

"Safe?" What is the matter with you, Bear?" Runt asked angrily. "We have no idea where we are. We've been seen by men who are plotting to kill Nephi. And now we're running for our lives from those same men, who want to kill us as well. How could we possibly be safe?"

"I meant, are we still being followed," Bear retorted heatedly. "I know we're not safe."

"We've got to find a place to hide, Stick," suggested Red. "We can't just wander around out here in the open. We're going to be seen."

"Or caught and killed," added Runt.

"I agree," replied Stick. "I'm just not sure where."

As the boys relaxed their pace, they searched for a safe place to hide. They wandered aimlessly, searching everywhere. About five minutes had passed when they heard someone yell from behind them.

"There they are! I found them!" called a man with a high, squeaky voice.

Without even turning around, the boys took off running full speed. Their hearts were beating so loudly that Stick was sure he could hear Bear's heart pounding behind him. Again, dodging in and out of alleys, around strange plants and trees, and buildings resembling Mayan temples, the boys frantically searched for a place to hide.

"Guys, look!" yelled Bear. "There's a small house or

something up in the distance. Whoever lives there might help us," he said as he ran toward the small, dimly-lit home.

"No, Bear, follow me," called Stick. "The men will check there. I'll think we'll be safer in the thick foliage just ahead."

Stick led the way further east into the city. He ran as fast as he could, but his legs were still not responding the way he thought they should. As the boys rounded the corner of a large building, Stick spotted nearly thirty woven baskets lined up against the wall of a large building.

"Quick, before we're seen. Find an empty basket, climb inside, and don't say a word. When the men are gone, I'll let you know," insisted Stick.

"What's inside them?" asked Runt.

"Who cares?" replied Red. He pulled several lids off the baskets, searching for one that was empty and tall enough to hide his entire body.

"Is this trash?" Runt asked, disgusted by the smell.

"Who care's, just get inside," demanded Stick, as he pulled the lid closed on his basket.

The rest of the boys quickly did the same just in the nick of time. Runt soon heard panting from their pursuers who were chasing after them. They were standing right next to the baskets where the boys were hiding.

"Did you see where they went?" asked Giddianhi.

"No, sir, I did not," replied the man with the high, squeaky voice.

"Ethem, did you find them?" demanded Giddianhi.

"No, sir. They vanished," he replied, as he bent over

and placed his hands on his knees, trying to catch his breath.

"They didn't just vanish. We must find them!" screamed Giddianhi. "We've got to find out what they heard."

"Sir, did you notice the clothes they were wearing? Or the packs they had strapped to their back?" asked Ethem. "I don't believe they were from our city."

"I saw them, too," said Morihan. "I think you're right. They did not look like they were from our city."

"Where do you think they're from?" asked Ethem.

"They must have been sent by the Lamanite King, Tubaloth, to try to take the City of Zarahemla," replied Giddianhi.

"Boys? King Tubaloth sent boys to capture our great city?" asked Morihan. "Why would the king send boys?"

"Maybe he believes we would not suspect children," replied Ethem.

"Maybe he sent boys to spy on us—not to over take our city. Then they can take back secrets about our army. We must advise Captain Gilead as soon as possible," said Giddianhi. "After we find these boys."

"Where is Lib?" asked Ethem. "Could he have found those boys?"

"No. I did not find them either," Lib replied, as he walked toward the group of men.

"Nor have I," said Shiz, following behind his brother Lib.

"What should we do?" asked Morihan.

"We continue to search. They've got to be here some-where," Giddianhi replied angrily. He drew his sword from underneath his cloak and wildly swung it, slicing the top off the basket Stick was hiding inside. Stick swallowed hard and scooted down in the basket, hoping the evil men did not see him. He listened nervously to the men continue to search. He was somewhat relieved, as the men's voices grew softer as they moved away from the boys.

Stick slowly moved his hand to the top of his head, checking to see if any of his hair was missing. "Wow, that was close," he thought to himself.

Finding none of his hair missing, he slowly inched his way up so he could see over the rim of the basket. He carefully looked around the area for any sign of the men.

"Runt!" Stick called in a soft voice. "Where are you?"

"I'm right here," Runt answered, slowly pushing the top off the basket.

"Red, Bear, where are you guys?" called Stick quietly.

"I'm here," replied Red. Are you all right?"

"Yeah, that was close though. For a minute, I was afraid that I was missing some of my hair."

"You're lucky you aren't missing some of your head," teased Runt.

"Where is Bear?" asked Stick. "Which basket is he hiding in?"

"I didn't see which basket he climbed into," whispered Red. "I bet he's afraid to come out."

"I don't blame him," replied Runt. "I'm not too excited to be out in the open either."

"Should we just stay hidden inside these baskets?" asked Red.

"They would eventually find us," said Stick. "And I

wasn't sure I could stand the smell inside mine much longer."

"Me neither," agreed Runt. "I smell like fish."

Stick laughed quietly and said, "Help me find which basket Bear is hiding in, and then let's get out of here—before those men come back."

"Bear, come on. Quit messing around. We don't have time for this," insisted Red, as he started to pull the lids off each basket.

"Bear, the men are gone. Let's go," urged Runt, searching the baskets as well.

"Bear! Bear!" called Stick. "We've got to get out of here."

"Where did he go?" asked Red, as he pulled the last lid off. "He's not inside any of these baskets."

"Look again," insisted Stick. "He's got to be here somewhere."

"Where could he have gone?" asked Runt, confused as to why they could not find Bear. "He was running with us. I tripped on his foot and told him to hurry up."

"There they are!" yelled Morihan. "Ethem, Lib, I can see them."

The men started running from the end of the street toward the boys.

With Bear no where in sight, Stick yelled, "Runt, Red, come on. We will find him later. We've got to go. If we get caught, we'll never be able to find him."

Runt tentatively agreed, and squealed, "I don't want to leave him, but follow me."

Running east again, the boys tried to stay in the

shadows of the buildings and foliage. They weaved between buildings and structures, trying to confuse the men by backtracking over their footprints several times. They eventually worked their way toward the wilderness in the distance. Nervous about leaving Bear they continued to whisper his name everywhere they ran.

"I don't like this. I don't want to leave Bear. I think we should go back and look for him," Red called gasping for breath, as he looked over his shoulder back in the direction they had come.

"We will, but we've got to find a safe place to hide first," reasoned Stick.

"I wouldn't want you to leave me," Red angrily responded.

"We're not leaving him," insisted Stick heatedly. "We'll find him as soon as we can."

"Do you think those men caught him?" asked Runt, breathing heavily.

"No. I don't think so. When we were hiding in the baskets and the men were talking, they hadn't found any of us?" reassured Stick. "So, I think we've just been separated."

"I sure hope so, Stick," replied Runt in a crackling voice. "You know we would never leave him here in *Book of Mormon* times. So, we're not going home without him!"

"I'm sure we're going to find him, so relax," insisted Stick. "You know we would never leave anyone."

"I can see some smoke from chimneys up ahead. Should we try to hide there?" asked Runt, completely out of breath. "I've got to stop."

"We've got to try," replied Red. "I can't run anymore."

"We could try, but we better be careful," suggested Stick, as the boys entered a small clearing. "We don't know who's got those fires lit."

"Look!" roared Red, startling Stick and Runt.

"Ssshhhh quiet, Red," said Stick. "You're gonna get us caught."

"What? Look where?" asked Runt, frightened the men could be close.

"There's a boy in the doorway of that barn. He's waving for us to follow him," replied Red. "Can you see him?"

"Yeah, I can see him. Do you think it's safe?" asked Stick suspiciously.

"If it is a trap, it's not going to be any worse than if we're caught by those men," replied Red, nervously looking over his shoulder.

"What if it is those men, are making that boy try to get us to come up there?" asked Stick.

"What if it's not and that boy is really trying to help us?" asked Red, slowly walking toward the barn.

"We've got to get out of the open. I'm afraid we're going to be seen," said Runt, anxiously.

"Follow him then," said Stick. "Maybe he can help us. But if it's a trap, it's not my fault."

"Whether it's safe or not, I've got to sit down for a minute," said Red. "I can hardly breathe. I feel like I'm going to have a heart attack."

"All right, all right," Stick reluctantly agreed. "If we've got to stop, we'll stop."

Red, Runt and Stick moved quickly toward the boy.

He motioned for them to follow him inside what looked to be a barn. They cautiously wiggled through the door and disappeared into the darkness.

Chapter Five

Once inside, the boys scanned their surroundings looking for the boy. They hoped they had not just walked into a trap. The door unexpectedly closed, startling them. They spun around to see a small hand snap the door latch closed. Suddenly, they were face to face with the tall, thin, dark-haired, teenage boy.

"Come, follow me, quickly. You're not safe here," the boy said.

He glanced at their strange clothes and then quickly turned, motioning for the boys to follow.

The teammates followed him without saying a word, grateful for his help. As they maneuvered around the many animals, they stopped just before reaching the back wall. The boys watched as their new friend placed a ladder through an opening in the ceiling of the barn. The boys stared at the wobbly, wooden ladder, surprised as the boy motioned for them to climb.

"There's an area in the loft filled with straw. Hide inside the straw, and do not leave the barn until I call for you. Be sure not to come down out of the loft unless I tell you to. It is a matter of life and death for you and me," the boy warned. "Don't make a sound. Now hurry, and get into the loft."

"Why are you helping us?" asked Runt, skeptical of the boy's help.

"I saw you running through the city from those men, and I thought you might be in danger," replied the boy. "Men dressed in black robes chasing children doesn't seem quite right to me."

"How could you see us from here?" asked Red, unsure whether or not to believe the boy's explanation.

"On the west wall of the loft is an opening where hay and straw are lifted into the stable. At night, when I am all alone, I sit by the opening and stare at the grand city of Zarahemla. Then I don't feel so lonely," the boy explained, as he again motioned for the boys to climb into the loft. "Now, if you do not want to be killed, get up there and hide yourselves," the boy instructed.

With that, he turned and left the boys standing at the bottom of the ladder. Then he headed back toward the front of the stable.

"Wait! Can you tell me what year this is?" asked Stick.

"What year this is?" asked the boy, shocked at the question. "There is no time for questions now. The men chasing you are very close. Please climb into the loft and hide. It was not my plan to die tonight. Ask your questions later."

"Mine either," replied Runt, as he took a hold of the ladder and began to climb.

"I guess we better climb up there, then," said Stick. "Red, you go next after Runt, and I'll go last," he insisted.

Red and Runt started frantically climbing, afraid that the men could burst through the door and find them at any second. Only seconds passed before the boys had scaled the twenty steps to the top. Runt and Red waited for Stick to make his way to the top. Once there, they located the pile of straw on the floor. They quickly wiggled their bodies underneath the large stack until they were completely covered.

Suddenly, the boys heard the barn door squeak loudly as it was thrown open. Worried that the cloaked men might find them, Stick brushed the straw from his face. He quickly checked to make sure they had not left any tracks leading to the straw where they were hiding. Then he checked the straw to make sure all of their belongings were well covered. Satisfied, Stick again covered his face with straw and waited nervously.

"Caaann I help you?" asked the boy, pretending to be startled.

"Where are they, boy?" growled Giddianhi.

"Where are who, sir?" asked the boy. He continued to calmly brush the horse, acting confused by his question.

"Don't play with me, child. They had nowhere else to hide but in here," Giddianhi growled angrily.

"I'm sorry, sir. I don't know what you are talking about," replied the boy. "I am the only one here, and you are going to get me into trouble. My master does not allow strangers in his stable."

"I know they are here," bellowed Lib, as he scoured the area for any sign of the boys. "I can smell them."

"The only things you can smell in here are the animals," insisted the boy, scowling at the man. "As I said, my master does not allow me to have visitors in the barn."

"If no one is here besides you, then you won't mind if we take a look around," said Ethem, as he angrily pushed by the boy.

"No sir, I do not mind. But as I told you, my master, Captain Gilead, does not allow anyone else in his barn. He might mind that you are in here. You must first get his permission."

"Permission from the Captain?" hollered Giddianhi laughing. "Why would I need permission from him? I'm the Commander of Gilead's personal army."

"I'm sorry, sir," the boy said timidly. "I did not recognize you with the dark mark on your face. However, you still must have Captain Gilead's permission before you may enter."

Giddianhi stopped abruptly, remembering the dark cloak he was wearing. Realizing he should not be seen wearing the cloak in public, he nervously turned to the other men and said, "We must go. This boy works for our Captain. I'm sure he has not seen or helped anyone here tonight. I can tell by the way he has protected the Captain's animals that he would never break any of Gilead's laws. I commend you, son, for your loyalty. I will personally report to Captain Gilead tomorrow what a brave servant you are for standing up to my men when we tried to enter the Captain's personal stable."

Giddianhi turned abruptly toward the barn door and motioned for the men to follow.

"But Giddianhi, I have not searched the entire stable yet," yelled Shiz, as he stood with one foot on the loft ladder.

"They're not here, Shiz," yelled Giddianhi. "The boy has assured me that no one has entered here tonight. Right, son?" Giddianhi again asked, staring sternly into the boy's eyes.

"I do not know of whom you speak, but I can guarantee you that I am the only one in this stable Commander," assured the boy.

"That is good, son," replied Giddianhi. He and his men exited the barn, closing the door behind them and disappearing into the darkness outside.

The boy calmly picked up the horse's reigns and started to brush its beautiful, long, white mane with his fingers. With the sound of the men's voices gone from the stable, the teammates waited for the boy to call. Several minutes of silence passed with no word from him. Afraid something might be wrong, Stick could feel a knot of panic start to grow in his stomach.

"What is he doing down there?" Stick whispered impatiently. "Is everything okay?"

"He just saved our lives, Stick," replied Red. "He must know something. Give him a minute. Maybe he's just making sure the coast is clear. I'm sure everything is fine."

"I agree, Stick. I'm sure he knows what he's doing," said Runt. "Be patient."

"Red, are you in a position that you could see what's happening?" asked Stick.

"No, not really. But if you give me a second, I could easily move to the edge of the loft. Why?" asked Red.

"I think we should check on him. See if you can quietly move to the edge and see what's happening down there," Stick said.

Without a word, Red agreed and carefully wiggled his body out of the straw. He slithered on his stomach like a snake to the edge of the loft and peered over the side. Spotting the boy quickly, Red quietly watched as he brushed the horse's mane.

Red watched for several minutes as the boy calmly tended to the animal. Unexpectedly, the barn door flew open, slamming loudly into the back wall. Red gasped, startled by the noise. Glancing quickly toward the sound, he noticed a large man with long, black hair rushing through the door. Red instinctively pulled his head away from the ledge, hoping he had not been seen. He placed his hand on his heart, trying to calm the rapid beating, as he listened to the screams of the man below.

"What is going on in here, Tulio?" demanded the deep, booming voice. "Who has been in my private stable?"

Tulio calmly looked up and replied, "One of your commanders, Sir. He came in and wanted to look around."

"Why did you allow them to enter? You know my rules," Captain Gilead screamed. "No one is to enter my personal stable. No one!"

"The soldier demanded entrance and pushed me aside, Sir," explained Tulio, startled by Captain Gilead's reaction. "He told me that he was looking for someone."

"You know that no one is allowed in here, Tulio—No matter what," said Captain Gilead, as he calmly brushed his horse's mane. "You know that you're to report to me immediately if anyone should try to enter. I'm sure you don't want to be punished."

"No, Captain. I am sorry. I thought I could stop the men. I will not allow entrance again. The army Commander, Giddianhi, told me you would allow him entrance, and that he would report the incident to you immediately. I did not want to leave the stable unattended with his men inside, so I stayed. I apologize. I will not allow anything like this to happen again," replied Tulio.

"Well, Tulio, I do not care what the men said. I don't care if they are with my army, and I don't care if it is my son. No one, except you, may enter this stable without me being present. Do you understand what I have said?" asked Captain Gilead, staring angrily at the boy.

"Yes, Sir. I understand," Tulio replied quietly. "I will not allow it again."

"Good," replied Captain Gilead, as he took hold of Tulio's shirt and pulled him two inches from his face. "Then you understand if this happens again, you will lose your life?"

"Yyyeeessss, Captain. I understand," Tulio replied in a shaky voice.

Captain Gilead pushed Tulio to the ground as he released his shirt, patted the horse's nose and walked out of the stable. He headed toward the large Mayan-style temple about twenty yards to the east.

Red watched as the boy fell in a heap on the floor. The boy buried his head in his hands for several seconds, obviously overwhelmed by the stressful situation.

Quietly wiggling back toward the straw, Red whispered, "That kid just saved our lives, guys."

"Who was the man that was talking?" asked Runt.

"Some Captain. I don't recognize his name from the *Book of Mormon*," answered Red. "But he was really big and really mean."

"Do you have any idea what's wrong yet, Stick?" asked Red. "I'm ready to figure it out and get out of here."

"I have a couple ideas actually," Stick quietly whispered.

"What are they?" demanded Red, a little excited.

"Well, the men that are chasing us, we know they have captured and are holding a prisoner—someone they said was very important. I'm not sure who it is, but I think they were talking about a prophet. So, my first idea is that we need to find the prisoner and free him. Or, my second idea is that those men are planning to kill Nephi in three days, and we're here to save him from being killed."

"Did you recognize any of the names of the men chasing us?" asked Red.

"Yeah, I sure did. But only because I think they're funny names—like Shiz," interrupted Runt.

"I recognized Giddianhi and Shiz," answered Stick.

"They were both bad guys in the *Book of Mormon*."

"What did they do, Stick? I can't remember," said Runt.

"I can't remember, either. We're gonna to have to find their names in the *Book of Mormon* and read about them to find out," Stick replied quietly.

"Are the Lamanites or Nephites righteous during this time?" asked Runt. "Do we know yet?"

"Not for sure. I've got to check some dates in the *Book of Mormon,* and then I'll know for sure," replied Stick. "I'm not as familiar with the time during the Gadianton robbers as I am with other times in the *Book of Mormon*."

"Who is the Nephi that those men talked about killing?" asked Red. "Is he the Nephi spoken about in the beginning of the *Book of Mormon*?"

"His father, Lehi, could be the prophet they talked about kidnapping," reasoned Runt. "Are we in the beginning of *Book of Mormon* times? 'Cause if we are, I've read those chapters a lot, and I'm sure I could figure out what's going on and what we need to do."

"No, I'm sure we're not in the year 600 B.C. I believe the city of Jerusalem, where Lehi and his family departed from, was a desert area, and we're in a tropical area," replied Stick.

"Why can't we be in the year 600 B.C.?" asked Runt. "You could be wrong."

"You're right, I could be wrong. But I'm not, because the kid downstairs said something about being in the grand city of Zarahemla. The city of Zarahemla is not talked about until later in the *Book of Mormon*. I'm not sure when it is first mentioned, but I know for sure it's not talked about until a long time after Lehi and Nephi."

"Are there other guys in the *Book of Mormon* named Nephi?" Red asked without thinking.

"Well, duh, Red," teased Runt.

"Funny, Runt. I'm just not thinking clearly. Traveling in time is very stressful," Red snapped. "Now, tell me all about the other men that are named Nephi in the *Book of Mormon*."

"All right, Red. Several men named Nephi are talked about in the *Book of Mormon*," replied Stick. "Now we've just got to find out which Nephi those men were talking about."

"So, what are we gonna do, guys?" cried Runt. "I really, really wish we were at home. I don't want to do this anymore."

"Me, too, Runt. I want to go home, too. But we're not going home until we do what we were sent here to do. So, instead of whining about everything, we've got to figure out what we need to do, so that we can make it safely back home," Stick said firmly. "And I'm gonna need you two to be strong. We've got to find Bear, fix what's gone wrong here in *Book of Mormon* times, whatever that is, and find the time to figure out how to work the Liahona so that we can go home."

"I'm worried about Bear," Red admitted. "What are we going to do?"

"We're gonna have to go look for him," Stick replied calmly. "I'm not sure we'll be able to do that tonight, but we're going to search for him as soon as we are safe to do so. I'm afraid the men chasing after us would kill us if they caught us. We've got to be very careful."

"I don't want to die here, Stick," whispered Red.

"And neither do I," said Stick. "I think the best thing we can do is search for Bear in the morning and pray that he'll be safe until we can find him. Then, we will figure out how to get out of here before someone really gets hurt."

Chapter Six

The boys squirmed slowly out of their hiding places and climbed on top of the large pile of straw. They were afraid to be out in the open, but tired of hiding. Curious to see where they were, Runt crawled to the opening that overlooked the city. Hoping to see Bear wandering somewhere in the streets, he searched every inch of the area he could see.

He noticed lush, green foliage everywhere, and he was surprised to see flowers of every color, shape and size. Vines grew on the ground, up the sides of many buildings and from tree to tree, making a canopy of green. There were only a few people wandering through the city's streets. The river sparkled in the distance in the bright light of the moon, casting a beautiful, but mysterious, glow on the tops of the buildings.

Overwhelmed by everything that had happened, and unable to see Bear anywhere in the city streets, Runt laid his head on his arms and closed his eyes, wishing he were home in his nice, warm bed.

"Can you tell me who I just risked my life for?" demanded the teenage boy, startling Stick, Red and Runt, who had momentarily drifted off to sleep.

"Uumm, uumm, you risked your life for travelers from another place," replied Stick, unsure what to say.

"Travelers from another place? What does that mean?" asked the boy.

"I'm not sure you are going to believe us," answered Red, frightened by the boy's attitude.

"You had better make me believe, or I will find Giddianhi and tell him where you are," threatened the boy. "And he is not a nice man."

"We have been sent from the future to your time, to help the people here," said Runt.

"I do not believe you. How can you help my people, and what do they need help with?" asked the boy, still standing with one foot on the ladder and one foot on the loft floor.

"How do we explain this to him, Stick?" asked Runt, unsure what to do. "He's never going to believe us."

"May I ask your name?" asked Stick, looking at the boy.

He paused for a moment before he replied. "My name

is Tulio, although I do not know how that will help you."

"Tulio, my name is Stick. I have traveled to your land with the help of Heavenly Father and Jesus Christ, using an instrument called the Liahona."

"Where is the instrument you use? Let me see it," insisted Tulio.

Stick looked at Red nervously, then replied, "I don't have it right now."

"Lies. All you speak are lies!" yelled Tulio. He started down the ladder. "I will not be tricked. I put my life at risk tonight. The least you could do is be honest with me."

"No! Wait! I'm not lying to you. One of the boys that traveled with us was lost as we tried to escape from those men. He has the Liahona in his backpack," Stick explained.

Tulio paused and looked at Stick.

"I have my backpack. Let me show some of the things from my time," said Stick, as he slipped the pack off his shoulder. "Then you will know I am telling you the truth."

Tulio watched suspiciously as Stick unzipped Tater's backpack and started to unload the contents. He pulled out several candy bars, a roll of toilet paper, a Swiss army knife, twenty feet of rope, a *Book of Mormon*, a sweat-shirt, a pencil and two packs of chewing gum. There were more items in Tater's pack, but Stick hoped that he had enough to convince Tulio. He looked up at Tulio and asked, "Do you believe me now?"

"What are they? Why should I believe you?" barked Tulio. "I do not know what those things are."

Stick could see that Tulio had no idea what he had pulled from the backpack. Suddenly desperate, he picked up the *Book of Mormon* from the floor and said, "This book was written thousands of years ago. On its pages are the records that the prophets of your time wrote concerning your people."

"How did you get the records?" quizzed Tulio.

"The records were engraved on plates of gold or brass. Those records were kept safely hidden by the Lord in a mountainside until a man named Joseph Smith found the plates with the help of Moroni, an ancient prophet. The Lord told him to translate the records into our language for the people of our time, so that we might know of the things that happened in your time," replied Stick.

"That book you say is our record does not look like engraved plates to me," said Tulio. "You are speaking the same language as I am. Why would the records of my people need to be translated and written in another language? None of what you are saying makes sense."

"Actually, with the Lord's help we can speak your language, but most of our people speak another language. The records had to be translated into a language that most people could read," answered Red.

"Tulio, my name is Runt. Could I ask you one question, please?"

"What is it?" snapped Tulio.

"Can you tell me what year we are in right now," Runt requested. "We would understand better what we are here to do if we knew exactly where we were."

"Year?" questioned Tulio. "What do you mean by year."

"In our land, time is measured in years. Do you keep any sort of time here?" Runt asked.

"Time? Do you mean a calendar of our days?" asked Tulio.

"Yes, I mean a calendar of your days, how do you measure them?" asked Runt

"It is the eighty-sixth year of the Nephites," replied Tulio.

"Do we know what happened in this year, Stick?" asked Red.

"I'd have to look it up in the *Book of Mormon*," he answered. "I could find out pretty quick."

"With this book, Tulio, we can look to see what is supposed to happen in your day," said Red, as he picked up Stick's *Book of Mormon*.

"Why are all those things wet?" questioned Tulio.

"When we came here, we landed in the river," replied Runt.

"And we spent several hours there," added Red, holding up his wrinkled fingers to show Tulio.

"Then how did you get into the city dressed the way you are? The guards would never have let you enter looking the way you do," insisted Tulio.

"We were able to find a grate with a small opening into the city's water system that allowed us access inside. Then we followed the water tunnels that wind underneath the city, until we saw those men dressed in black. When they saw us, they started chasing us until you saved us," said Runt.

"You found the hidden tunnels of Zarahemla?" Tulio asked, surprised at Runt's words.

"We didn't know they were hidden," replied Stick. "We wanted to find a way into the city. But, dressed like this, we knew we would not be allowed to enter through the front gates."

"No, the guards would never have let you enter," agreed Tulio, in a somewhat relaxed voice. "But why were the men chasing you?"

"We overheard a conversation they were having in the tunnels. When they saw us, they started chasing us," answered Stick. "I guess they didn't want us to know what they were talking about."

"One of them even got close enough to grab my leg! I thought he had me for sure," added Red. "I'm sure that crazy guy would have killed me if he'd caught me."

"Yes, he probably would have killed you. Not only did you hear them, but I also believe you found part of the hidden tunnels of Zarahemla. They are spoken of often, but I have never met anyone who has been in them and lived to tell about it!" exclaimed Tulio. "Gadianton's men are the only ones who know where those tunnels are, or how to get inside. Are you sure you are not some of his men?"

"We've come to the time of the Gadianton robbers?" squealed Red. "Those are bad men. Stick, I want to go home. This isn't funny. I don't want to be here during the time of the Gadianton robbers."

"We don't have a choice, Red," replied Stick. "We're already here, and we don't get to go home until we figure out what the Lord needs us to do."

"Tulio, what exactly are the hidden tunnels?" asked Runt.

"From what I know, the tunnels are hidden underneath the city. Depending on which tunnel you take, it will lead you from one side of the city to the other. They also lead in and out of the city as needed. I've heard they lead to secret rooms where meetings are held. I was also told Gadianton's men even have rooms set up to hold prisoners.

"Anyway, the tunnels are where the Gadianton robbers hide their stolen treasures, hold prisoners, kill people and make plans to do bad things. But, I believe their main purpose is to provide those men with safe escape routes," answered Tulio. "Very few men know how to enter the tunnels. No wonder they want you three dead."

"Do you think they will continue to try and find us?" Runt asked nervously.

"Yes, they will continue to search for you until they find you. They will never stop looking for you until they are sure you are captured or dead," replied Tulio.

"Stick, we've got to find Bear. Hero won't be very happy if we don't bring his cousin home," said Runt.

"I know we've got to find him, Runt. But I don't think we should go out searching tonight. I think those men are gonna be searching the city all night trying to find us. I'm hoping that Bear was able to find a place to hide and that he will stay there until we can come for him," replied Stick.

"Tulio, when you saw us running from those men, you didn't happen to see where our friend went, did you?" asked Red. "He's a small guy—about four and a half to five feet tall, with blond hair and brown eyes."

"I did see that there were four of you running, but I did not see where your friend hid," answered Tulio.

"Are there places in the city where he could hide and be safe?" asked Runt. "Places where Gadianton robbers couldn't find him?"

"Most of the people here in Zarahemla are loyal to Captain Gilead—the man that I work for," Tulio replied. "But there are a few who are not, and would help your friend if they saw him."

"Are you one of the good guys?" asked Red.

Tulio, still standing on the ladder, softly replied, "I am as loyal as I have to be to Captain Gilead. I care for his personal animals and tend to his stable. But I am loyal to myself and my God first," he replied. "I only hope that you three are good guys."

"We are good guys," insisted Stick. "Who else would leave their own land to go and help wherever the Lord needs them?"

Without a word, Tulio smiled, then stepped from the ladder onto the floor of the loft and walked quietly toward the boys. He knelt down next to the contents of Tater's backpack and picked up the *Book of Mormon*. "Can you really read to me what the prophets wrote about our time?" he asked curiously.

"I can read to you everything that is written," replied Stick. "Would you like me to see if I can find the writings of your time?"

"Can you tell me if the things that happen in my time are good things?" asked Tulio.

"I don't know from memory what happened during your time, but I can look up the information and read it to you," answered Stick.

"I'm not sure if I want to know what happens in the future. But, if I decide that I would like to know, would you read it to me at a later time?" asked Tulio.

"Sure, you bet," replied Stick, smiling at Tulio's obvious interest.

"Can you tell me what the men were talking about in the tunnel?" asked Tulio. "Were you able to hear anything?"

"Yes. We heard that someone named Nephi is returning to the city in the next few days," said Red.

"Really? Nephi is returning to Zarahemla?" Tulio asked excitedly.

"That is what the men said," replied Red. "Who is Nephi?"

"Shouldn't you know the answer to that question?" Tulio asked skeptically.

"I would, if we were certain about the year," answered Stick.

"I believe Nephi is a prophet of God," said Tulio. "Does that help you?"

"No, not yet. What other information can you tell us?" asked Stick.

"Let's see...Nephi travels around, visiting all the surrounding cities. He teaches the word of God and calls upon the wicked to repent," replied Tulio. "Does that help?"

"That helps," replied Stick, as he flipped through the pages of the *Book of Mormon*. He located the chapter and verse that correlated with that time period. "I believe you are talking about Nephi the Second, eldest son of

Helaman, the Chief Judge," said Stick. "Is that correct?"

"Yes, it is. How did you know?" asked Tulio.

"From this book that we told you about," replied Runt. "Did you think we were joking?"

"Yes, a little. I don't know of anyone who has the knowledge that you have. The Lord has greatly blessed you."

"Yes, he has," agreed Stick.

Stick quickly scanned through the *Book of Mormon* chapters that referred to Nephi the Second, while Red and Runt explained to Tulio about the other articles Stick had pulled out of the backpack and laid on the floor.

"So, did the men say anything else in the tunnel?" asked Tulio.

"Anything like what?" asked Red. "Is there information you need?"

"I was just wondering," replied Tulio, dropping the subject.

"I get the feeling you are not telling me something, Tulio," said Runt.

"I was hoping they might give the location of a missing prophet," he replied. He held the candy bar to his nose, sniffing the strange smells of chocolate and caramel.

"Didn't they say something about a prisoner, Stick?" asked Red. "I thought you said they mentioned something about a prisoner."

"Yeah, they said something about Nephi coming to look for a missing prophet, or something like that," replied Stick.

"Did they mention his name?" asked Tulio, anxious for the answer.

"No, I don't remember them mentioning a name," answered Red.

"Me neither. I don't remember any of them talking about who the prophet was," agreed Runt.

"I know who it is," Stick squealed excitedly, holding up the *Book of Mormon.*

"Who the Gadianton robbers are holding captive?" asked Runt.

"I think so. Listen to this and tell me what you think. In Helaman chapter ten, verse seventeen, it reads,

"'And it came to pass that thus he did go forth in the Spirit, from multitude to multitude, declaring the word of God, even until he had declared it unto them all, or sent it forth among all the people.'

"I think that confirms what Tulio said Nephi is doing, traveling around and preaching to everyone," said Stick, excited at the possibility of learning where they were for sure. "Then in Helaman chapter sixteen, verse one, it reads,

"'And now, it came to pass that there were many who heard the words of Samuel, the Lamanite, which he spake upon the walls of the city. And as many as believed on his word went forth and sought for Nephi; and when they had come forth and found him they confessed unto him their sins and denied not, desiring that they might be baptized unto the Lord.'"

"Doesn't that sound right?" asked Stick.

"Are you saying we're here during the time of Samuel the Lamanite?" Red asked nervously.

"That's what I think. I think the prophet those men were speaking about is the only Lamanite Prophet spoken of in the *Book of Mormon*—Samuel the Lamanite," insisted Stick.

"Tulio, do you know anything about a man named Samuel the Lamanite?" asked Runt.

"Yes, I have heard of a man called Samuel the Lamanite," replied Tulio.

"Has he preached the word of God on the great wall in the city yet?" Red asked excitedly.

"Not that I know of," replied Tulio. "But I don't think he will ever be able to do that in this city. I don't think Gadianton's men would ever allow him to do that here. They have chased him away from the city before when he's tried to preach the word of God. I'm sure they would kill him if he tried to preach on top of the wall."

"Runt, Red, are you thinking what I'm thinking?" asked Stick excitedly, looking up from the *Book of Mormon*.

"I'm not sure," said Red. "What are you thinking?" he asked with a smile.

"I bet we're here for one of two reasons. Either we are here to keep Nephi safe from the men who plan to kill him in a few days, or we're here to find the prophet that the Gadianton's are holding prisoner, and help free him so that he can climb on the wall and give the message the Lord would have him give," said Stick.

"How will we figure out which is the right idea, Stick?" asked Red.

"I don't know. But, I do know that there could be more than one thing that needs to be fixed in this time period," replied Stick. "We may just have to do them both."

"How do we do that?" asked Runt. "I don't understand."

"Well, I think we're going to have to find Nephi and make sure that those men aren't able to kill him. We are also going to have to make our way back into the hidden tunnels and find the prophet who the Gadianton robbers are holding captive," said Stick.

"And one of us is going to have to search for Bear," added Red. "How are we going to do all of those things at once?"

"Maybe we'll have to get Tulio's help," answered Runt, smiling at their new friend.

"I have been sneaking out every night for more than a week searching for the prophet. It is because of him that I have repented and been baptized," said Tulio. "I would love to help you find him, but only after I get some sleep. I'm tired," he replied.

"We are very blessed to have found you, Tulio," said Red. "I'm not sure we would still be alive without your help."

"No, I am the blessed one. You are an answer to my prayers. I've asked the Lord every night for a week for help to find the prophet," Tulio replied. He found an empty area of straw, fluffed it up and plopped down. "I must get some sleep tonight. The hour is late, and I've got chores to do early in the morning."

"Is this where you sleep?" asked Stick.

"Yes. Will this straw be okay for all of you?" he asked nervously.

"Yes, the straw will be perfect. Thank you," replied Runt.

"Tulio, before you go to sleep, tell me something. Are you a Nephite or a Lamanite?" asked Red.

"I'm one of the few righteous Nephites in the city of Zarahemla," he replied. "Now, I will see you in the morning. If you need anything, wake me. Do not leave the stable, your lives as well as mine would be in danger," Tulio insisted.

The teammates watched as he laid his head down in the straw and quickly fell asleep.

Chapter Seven

The boys sat quietly, pondering all the trouble they were going to be in when they returned home. Runt thought about the lawn he had put off mowing for almost two weeks. He only had until tomorrow to mow it before he would be grounded for a week. Starving, Red thought about all the great things back home that he could be eating. Stick, worried about Tater and all the stress he had to deal with, as he remembered everything Tater did while Hero, KP, Bean and Bubba were gone. But mostly, the three boys were thinking about where they were in the *Book of Mormon*.

"Do you really think that we're in the time of Samuel the Lamanite?" Runt asked quietly.

"I do," replied Stick.

"I can't believe all of this!" Red said excitedly. "I wish I knew more about the time of Samuel the Lamanite. All I know is that he gave a speech from the top of a wall and was protected while he did so."

"I know that the Nephites were wicked and the Lamanites were righteous during this time," added Runt.

"We're going to have to be very careful, because the Nephites are wicked. We're going to have a hard time determining who is a friend and who's not," said Stick.

"I'm starving, Stick! Did Tater have any other food besides candy bars in his backpack?" asked Red.

"I don't know. Let me check," Stick replied, as he picked up the backpack, unzipped the pocket and started rummaging through the contents. "There are more candy bars, gum, granola bars, a few crackers, and a small bag of pretzels. I'm sure there's more in here, but I'll have to unload everything else to see. Does any of that sound good?" Stick asked, looking up at Red.

"Keep looking for me, will you please? I was hoping he had a Twinkie or something like that," Red said as he watched Stick continue to unload Tater's backpack.

"I can't believe everything that Tater carries in here," said Stick, as he pulled another roll of toilet paper from the bag.

"Well, at least he put the toilet paper in a plastic bag. Even though our packs are wet, the paper inside is still useable. That was good thinking. Toilet paper could come in really handy for us," Runt whispered, not wanting to wake up Tulio.

"Hey, look what I found!" exclaimed Stick, holding up the walkie-talkie.

"Do you think it works?" Red asked excitedly, taking it from Stick's hand.

"It worked when Hero called home," answered Stick, as he shrugged his shoulders. "I can't see why it wouldn't work for us. Besides, it can't hurt to try."

"Wait a minute. You probably shouldn't turn it on until everything dries out," suggested Runt, as he took the walkie-talkie from Red.

"Serious?" questioned Red. "We can't use the walkie-talkie until it dries out?"

"We could try, but we might end up shorting it out," replied Runt.

"I don't think we want to do that!" said Stick. "I'd rather wait until it dries out. It shouldn't take that long."

"How long is it gonna take?" Red asked, obviously disappointed.

"I don't know for sure, but I can't imagine it will take too long," replied Stick.

"Hey, Stick, you don't happen to have the Liahona inside that backpack with everything else, do ya?" Red asked, already knowing the answer.

"Can I tell you how bad I wish I'd taken it from Bear earlier?" replied Stick, shaking his head in frustration. "I should have made him give it to me."

"I don't think having the Liahona will help us to get home faster," said Red. "It's not like we could have used it without Bear. And we haven't solved whatever problems there are that we need to yet, so that we can go home anyway."

"Didn't Hero and Bubba say something about the Liahona after they got home from their adventure?" asked Runt, with a look of contemplation on his face.

"Like what?" asked Stick. "The only thing I can remember them talking about is Captain Moroni and Lehi."

"I thought Bubba said the Liahona had a clue to the problem that they needed to fix, a scripture or something—that helped them figure out what they needed to do," said Runt.

"I didn't hear him say that," replied Stick.

"I'm sure of it," insisted Runt. "Bubba told me that if they had known the Liahona gave them a clue to what the problem was, they would have been able to come home earlier."

"Now that you mention it, I think you're right. I remember Bubba talking about that, too," agreed Red.

"He said something about how the Liahona changes or something, but I can't remember," Runt replied.

"What about the clue that the librarian, Cheri, translated for us while they were stuck on their adventure? Didn't it tell us what to do?" questioned Red.

"Oh, I think you're right! I can't remember exactly how the clue read, though. Let me think for a minute," mumbled Runt, as he paced back and forth, trying to remember.

"I wish I would've paid more attention. Those clues could come in handy right now," said Red.

"Hey, didn't Tater have Cheri's translation written on a paper in his backpack?" asked Stick. "I bet it's in here with everything else."

Unable to find the paper, Stick picked up the pack and dumped the contents on the floor.

"Is this it?" asked Red, snatching a paper from the ground and quickly unfolded it.

"Let me see!" said Runt, trying to take the paper from Red's hand.

"That's Tater's handwriting!" Stick exclaimed excitedly.

"Read it. Is it the clue?" Runt asked.

Stick looked at the paper, smiled and then started to read the clue to himself. Red and Runt watched Stick, waiting several moments for him to read the clue out loud, but he never did.

"Stick, we're waiting! Read it out loud already!" demanded Red.

Stick finally looked up and said, "Oh, sorry!"

Trying to be dramatic, he stood up, cleared his throat and held the paper at arms length. "Okay, let me see here. The clue Tater has written down starts with,

"Clue one–
'As you travel in time, doing service for the Lord,
Your knowledge will be tested, your return is the reward.
Take heed in the Lord's promptings, and remain faithful in all things.
The Liahona will direct you providing the answers you will need.

The Book of Mormon is your guide, at your side
    shows you the light.
Keep it with you as you journey, setting back what is
    not right.'

"Clue two—
'Your travels will begin when you hold treasure in your
    hand.
Be prepared to take a journey into a long-lost land.
Three flashes start your mission—your adventure to
    the past.
Without guidance from the Lord, your journey will
    forever last.'

"Clue three—
'Once your journey is through, and you've completed
    the task.
Then hold the Liahona, and you will travel straight
    back.
To the time you have left, you will most definitely
    return.
With the Lord's service finished, you will have no
    concern.
If the task is not complete, nowhere will you travel.
What's wrong must be right, or your history will unravel.
Your time it is short, your journey only seven of the
    Lord's days,
To fix what's gone wrong, or remain forever there to
    stay.'"

"So, what do we need to do?" asked Red.

"Exactly what we've done with all the other clues. Break them down line by line and solve them," replied Stick.

"'As you travel in time, doing service for the Lord. Your knowledge will be tested, your return the reward,' read Runt. "We've traveled in time, we're doing service right now, our knowledge is being tested and hopefully we'll return. Okay, what's next?"

"We need to listen to promptings from the Lord, stay faithful, and the Liahona will give us the answers that we need to solve the problems. I can do that," added Red. "I just need to listen better!"

"That's the understatement of the year," Runt teased.

"Let's keep working on the clue, guys," insisted Stick. He began working on the next part of the clue. "The *Book of Mormon* will guide us. We've just got to keep it with us as we try to figure out why the Lord needs us here," said Stick. "And our travels did begin when we held the treasure. We disappeared to a long lost land—just like the clue is written."

"The three flashes did start us on our mission, and we are most definitely on an adventure to the past," Red joked. "Although, I'm not sure this is exactly what I had in mind when I agreed to take a closer look at the Liahona."

Stick smiled and said, "Hind sight is always twenty-twenty, isn't it?"

"Yep, it sure it," agreed Red.

"In the next line, the clue refers to guidance from the Lord. That is the second time it has mentioned that we need to listen to the Lord's promptings. What does that mean exactly?" asked Runt.

"I think the clue is warning us to be responsive to the promptings of the Holy Ghost, refer to the scriptures when needed, and depend on the Lord for guidance, or we're going to be here in this land forever," Red replied matter-of-factly.

"The last clue tells us that once our journey is through and the tasks set forth by the Lord are completed, all we need to do is hold the Liahona and we will return to our time," said Runt.

"I'm a little concerned about the next verse," said Stick, reading through the clue.

"What do you mean?" asked Red.

"Well, if we don't correct the problem in this land, we won't get to travel home, and history as we know it will totally fall apart," answered Stick.

"I think we can figure out the problem, and I believe that we have the knowledge and ability to correct it. What worries me is the amount of time that we have to accomplish everything," Runt said worriedly.

"We have seven days," replied Red. "Don't you think that we can solve this in less than a week?"

"We don't have seven days, Red," said Runt. "We have seven of the Lord's days—whatever that means. And since we don't know exactly how long that is, we could run out of time."

"Stick, do you know how long seven of the Lord's days actually give us?" asked Red, a little shaken by Runt's comments.

"No, Red, I don't. I don't think anyone knows exactly how long the Lord's days are."

"Well then, I guess we better hurry and fix whatever has gone wrong in this time," suggested Red, timidly smiling. "'Cause I really, really, really don't want to be stuck here forever."

"Stick, I have a question," said Runt.

"What?" asked Stick, as he checked the contents of Tater's backpack to see if they were dry.

"Did Hero ever tell you how he was able to talk and understand the language spoken?" asked Runt.

"Yeah, he figured that the Lord gave them the gift of tongues while they were fixing the problems in the land," Stick replied.

"So, is that why we can speak to Tulio in English and it sounds like he's answering in English?" questioned Runt.

"I think so," Stick answered. "And I bet when Tulio talks to us he hears us respond in his language, although we're really answering in English."

"I'm glad he can understand us. Traveling in time would be horrible if we had no idea what was being said," responded Red.

"I agree," replied Stick. "Did you guys want something to snack on from Tater's food stash before I put it away?" he asked.

Runt found some jerky, and Red found a Twinkie, some peanuts and a granola bar.

"Hopefully Tulio will know where we can get some real food in the morning," said Runt.

"I hope so," said Stick, as he fluffed up the straw and

laid down his head. "I'm tired, guys. I'm gonna try to get some sleep."

"I've got to get some sleep, too," agreed Red, as he took another bite of the granola bar and snuggled into the straw.

"Me, too," replied Runt. "I've been watching out of the opening up here, and no one has moved in the city for more than an hour now. I think we're safe for tonight."

"Be careful what you say," warned Stick. "I don't want to jinx this mission before we even get started."

"Do you have any idea what time it is?" asked Red, as he stared out at the stars in the sky.

"No, but I sure wish I did know what time it was," answered Stick.

"Based on the activity in the city, I'm betting it's at least two or three in the morning," suggested Red.

"Yeah, I bet you're right. No wonder I'm so tired," said Runt as he dozed in and out of consciousness.

"Do you think one of us should stay up and keep watch tonight?" asked Red.

"Tulio doesn't seem to be to worried about anything," answered Stick. "So, I think we're probably all right to sleep."

"I'm worried about Bear, Stick. Do you think he's okay?" asked Red.

"He's pretty scrappy. I'm sure he's alright," replied Stick.

"He seemed pretty scared to me," said Runt sleepily.

"I can't figure out where he went," said Stick. "He was there, and then suddenly, he was gone."

"Do you think he has to sleep outside tonight?" asked Red, concerned for his friend's safety.

"I don't know. I hope not. That would be scary," admitted Runt.

"I can hear all the jungle noises in here, and they make me nervous," said Red.

"You know, we're here doing service for the Lord. I'm sure He will protect Bear," replied Stick.

"Are you sure?" asked Red.

"The clues tell us to be faithful," replied Stick. "We've just got to have faith that we'll find him and everything will be okay."

"Should we try to call home tonight or wait until morning?" asked Red.

"Do we know if it's the same time here as it is back home?" asked Stick. "I don't know how time works between home and *Book of Mormon* times."

"I don't know. I guess it could be the same time back home," replied Runt. "I'm not sure."

"I don't know. Hero said they were in *Book of Mormon* times for several days," replied Stick. "But back at home, they weren't even gone a full day."

"We better not try to call this late. We might blow whatever cover they have come up with for why we're not there," said Stick. "And the walkie-talkie is still wet. We better wait until morning to use it."

Red sat in the straw, holding his stomach. He was nervous because they did not know where Bear was, but he was even more nervous because their teammates back home did not know if they were all right.

"Don't worry, Red. The walkie-talkie will be dry in the morning. As soon as we find Bear, we'll call home and tell Hero that we're all okay!" reassured Stick.

"If we're going out early to look for Bear, then I'm getting some sleep," said Runt, as he fluffed up the straw.

"Me, too," replied Stick.

Red smiled and said, "I'm gonna sit here a few minutes before I go to sleep."

"Don't stay up too long. I want to start searching for Bear early," said Stick. He laid his head on the straw and quickly fell asleep.

Chapter Eight

Bear pulled his legs in tight to his body, as he slowly tugged a small blanket from the back of the wooden rocker. Covering everything but his eyes with the blanket, Bear tried to distinguish the shadows through the window of the dark cottage. Grateful no one was home, but nervous he would be found at any minute, he wished his friends had seen him sneak into the house.

Suddenly, he was startled by noises made by the men rummaging through the wicker baskets outside. Bear's hands shook uncontrollably. He strained to hear every word said by the men standing outside the window. He was relieved when he heard one of the men say that none of the spies had been caught yet.

As he watched the men finally walk off into the distance, he breathed a guarded sigh of relief. He nervously pulled the blanket away from his face and laid it on the ground. Then he cautiously crawled to the window, quickly took hold of the ledge and peered out into the darkness. Unable to see very well, he took the sleeve of his shirt and rubbed a small circle on the window pane.

"This isn't glass," he thought to himself as he rubbed. "I wonder what this is?"

Three shadows suddenly appeared outside the window. Bear quickly dropped to his knees and out of sight.

"The guards are back," he thought. "They must know I'm in here."

Several tense minutes passed before he dared to peek over the widow sill again.

"The shadows are gone again," he sighed. "I've got to get out of here."

Kneeling by the window, Bear turned to crawl toward the cottage door.

"Who are you?" an elderly man asked, startling Bear. "Why are you in my house?"

Frightened he was one of the men who had been chasing them, Bear stood quickly, but was too afraid to respond.

"Answer me, boy!" the man yelled. "Why are you in my home?"

"I...I...I was hiding, sir," Bear replied in a shaky voice.

"Hiding from whom? And why in my house?" he demanded gruffly.

As Bear looked into the dark-brown eyes of the man, he replied, "There were men chasing me."

"What men?" asked the man.

"Men in dark clothes," Bear quietly replied.

"Dark clothes?" he asked as he scratched his head, baffled by the description.

"Yes, sir. The men were wearing dark cloaks and had their faces covered."

"Oh," he replied, rubbing his chin.

"Do you know who they are?" Bear asked innocently.

"Yes," replied the man. "I know who they are."

Bear watched as the man moved slowly toward the rocking chair, where he had found the blanket. As he man sat down, the soft moonlight shone through the window and cast a pale light onto the man's face. Bear squinted as his eyes adjusted to the light. When his eyes finally focused, he gasped when he saw the man's face.

Bear ran frantically toward the cottage door, but the man jumped from the chair and blocked his way.

"Oh, you're not going anywhere, boy," said the man.

"Let me out of here, or I will scream," warned Bear, nervously backing away from the man.

"Go ahead and scream," said the man. "Only my men will hear you."

"No! My friends will save me," Bear insisted.

"We've already caught your friends, boy," claimed the man. He walked toward Bear, forcing him against the wall.

"No you haven't," cried Bear.

"You might as well give up, boy. No one is going to save you," said the man, as he lunged toward Bear, grabbing for his arm.

"Never!" screamed Bear, as he ducked under the

man's outstretched arm. He scrunched his little body down, dove, and rolled between the man's legs.

"You will never catch me!" he yelled, as he grabbed the door and quickly escaped into the darkness.

Back on the street, Bear quickly scanned the area. In front of him, about one hundred yards in the distance, he could see several men walking his way. To his left and rear were several buildings. To his right were scattered buildings that looked like homes, followed by the thick foliage of the jungle.

Suddenly the man from the cottage threw open the door and yelled, "I've got one of them! Ethem, Shiz, Lib, help me!"

Horrified of being captured, Bear sprinted toward the jungle. He hoped the trees and vines might provide a temporary hiding place until Stick, Runt and Red could find him.

"As long as they haven't already been captured," he said to himself, as he ran further into the darkness.

Bear ran for a long time, constantly looking over his shoulder. As he weaved in between the cottages and headed toward the foliage of the jungle, he had completely lost all sense of direction. Exhausted and overwhelmed by the situation, he fell to the ground in a heap and started to cry.

"Why am I here?" he thought to himself. "What did I do to deserve this?"

He laid on the ground for several minutes. Hearing a noise in the distance, he remembered he was being followed and knew he needed to find a place to hide. He took a deep breath, wiped the tears from his eyes, picked himself up from the ground and brushed the dirt and grass off his clothes.

He glanced around the area and quickly located a small willow tree with hundreds of hanging branches and leaves. He smiled as he remembered the hanging leaves on the Treehouse back home, and he knew the small willow tree could provide some shelter. Pushing the leaves aside, he quickly moved under the branches of the tree. Still breathing rapidly from running, he sat down and replayed the events that had just transpired in his mind.

"Where could everyone be?" he thought worriedly. "Why didn't they follow me?"

He sat for several minutes before he remembered that he had the Liahona inside his backpack.

"I wonder if it will tell me where everybody is," he thought, as he unzipped the pocket. He located the Liahona inside and carefully removed it from the bag. He gazed angrily at the small ball and thought, "What did you do to me?"

He noticed the intricate designs shift and the small panel flash Helaman chapter five, verse forty-seven. Excited to read the verse, he set the Liahona back inside his backpack and rummaged around for his scriptures. After several moments of frantic searching, he finally found the small book.

He flipped through the pages of his Book of Mormon looking for Helaman chapter five verse forty-seven. As soon as he found the correct scripture, he started reading.

"'Peace, peace be unto you, because of your faith in my Well Beloved, who was from the foundation of the world.'"

Bear took a deep breath as a tear trickled down his face. He thought about everything he had said in anger. Reflecting on the scripture he had just read, he laid his head on his backpack and listened to the sounds of the jungle.

"The sound of chirping crickets is so loud," Bear thought to himself. He cupped his hands over his ears, trying to soften the noise. "I'm never going to fall asleep."

A sleepless hour passed before Bear finally started to dose-off. Suddenly he was jolted from his sleep as he heard several voices just outside his willow tree hideout. He sat up quietly and listened to every word.

"We can't be seen dressed like this, Ethem!" said Giddianhi. "The sun will be rising soon. We've got to change."

"What about those spies?" asked Lib. "We haven't captured any of them."

"Let's put the word out to the citizens in the morning to watch for strangers in the city," suggested Shiz.

"Good idea," said Giddianhi. "If we do, I'm sure those spies will be caught in a matter of hours."

"Do we continue searching tonight?" asked Ethem.

"No," replied Giddianhi. "Let's get changed and wait until morning to continue the search."

"The boy I almost caught in the cottage has got to be somewhere close," protested Morihan, not wanting to give up. "Are you sure you don't want to continue looking tonight?"

"Yes! Let's get changed and continue in the morning," Giddianhi insisted, as the men started to walk back into the city.

Bear breathed a cautious sigh of relief as he watched the men disappear into the distance. Feeling safe momentarily, he laid his head on his backpack and fell asleep instantly.

※

Bear woke up early, determined to find his friends. He pulled the branches of the tree to the side and carefully poked his head out, checking to see if the area was safe. With no one in sight, he crawled out of his hiding spot. He grabbed his backpack, threw it over his shoulder, and cautiously started walking toward the city.

"I wish I could remember where I lost Stick, Red and Runt. I bet they're are still there looking for me. In fact,

I'm sure they were worried sick all night long," he thought to himself, smiling slightly.

Bear wandered slowly toward the city, cautiously moving between the buildings and trees, trying to stay hidden in the shadows. As he reached the market, he stared at everyone busily buying and selling their wares. He searched each face intently, hoping for any sign of his friends. Finding them nowhere in sight, he moved closer to the market. Hiding in the bushes, he hoped to hear what the people were saying.

"Giddianhi, may I speak with you?" asked the man, timidly looking down at the ground.

"What?" yelled Giddianhi, annoyed by the man's presence.

"I was wondering if the stories I heard in the market today are true?" asked the man.

"Stories?" questioned Giddianhi.

"Yes, sir," the man replied. "Stories of oddly dressed boys or visitors from outside our city?"

"What have you heard?" asked Giddianhi.

"That there is a substantial reward for anyone who can give information as to their whereabouts," the timid man replied.

"Have you seen them?" Giddianhi asked eagerly.

"I believe so," replied the man.

"Quit wasting my time!" scolded Giddianhi. "If you have seen them, then show me where they are!"

"I've only seen one boy," replied the man. "If I take you, will I receive a reward?"

"For one boy?" asked Giddianhi.

"Yes, sir," answered the man. "Is he worth anything?"

Giddianhi looked at Ethem and smiled mischievously. "I will decide after you show me where the boy is hiding," he said. "Show me now, before it is you that I am angry with."

The man knew he had no choice but to show Giddianhi and Ethem where the boy was hiding. Distraught, he turned toward the market and said, "If you will follow me, sir, I will take you to where I spotted the boy."

"How long ago did you see him?" asked Ethem.

"Only about ten minutes ago," the man replied quietly.

"He better still be there!" screamed Giddianhi. "If he has already moved on, you will be paying me a substantial reward."

The men quickly walked through the streets, easily maneuvering through the hundreds of people. After entering the market, the man turned and headed south.

"Where is he? Where are we going?" demanded Giddianhi.

"I saw him hiding in these weeds, sir," replied the man.

"It looks like he is gone, Giddianhi," said Ethem, as

they watched the man rustle through the bushes.

"If you hadn't worried about the reward, we would have caught him!" yelled Giddianhi, as he pulled his sword from its sheath.

"I'm very sorry, sir," the man said apologetically, looking to the ground. "He's got to be close."

"You had better find him," replied Giddianhi. "Or you better pray to the Gods for mercy from me!"

"Look, Giddianhi!" yelled Ethem. "There's the boy!"

"Where? Where?!" Giddianhi screamed anxiously.

"There, right there!" Ethem replied, pointing. "By the Elephant Ear bush."

"Hurry! Go catch him!" ordered Giddianhi, as he waved his sword high in the air.

Chapter Nine

The sun shone through the opening in the loft, directly onto Red's face. Still sleeping, he angrily swung at the light, trying to turn it off.

"Come on, Mom. I'm tired! Can I sleep a few more minutes?" he asked, squeezing his eyes closed tightly. "I didn't sleep very good last night. I had bad dreams all night long."

Surprised that his mom had not responded, he held his hand up to shield his eyes, and slowly opened them to see what she was doing. As he searched the area, he was confused why his mom was nowhere to be found.

"Mom?" called Red, nervously scanning the area. "Mom, are you here?"

"Your mom's not here, Red, you goof!" answered Runt. He sat up, fluffed the straw around him, and plopped back down. "Remember, we're on an adventure in *Book of Mormon* times. Now go back to sleep."

Red slowly sat up and tried to look around. Unable to focus on his surroundings, he rubbed his eyes several times. Then he shook his head, trying to clear the cobwebs. Stretching his eyes open as wide as he could, they finally started to focus. As he saw the pile of straw Runt was sleeping on, he suddenly remembered the crazy events of the previous day. Trying to distinguish between dreams and reality, Red nervously looked around the loft, hoping to find Bear and Stick. He quickly located Stick, asleep in the straw next to Runt, but there was no sign of Bear anywhere.

"I guess I wasn't having a bad dream," he thought to himself, as he shook his head back and forth. "I was living a bad dream!"

No longer sleepy, Red crawled to the edge of the loft and cautiously peered over the side looking for Tulio. Red noticed the beautiful white horse Tulio had meticulously brushed the night before. He also saw several chickens scattered around, a brown and white cow tied in a stall, a large brown pig, a horse saddle, bridle, and a lot of hay. Hanging on the wall to the right of the front door were several stretched skins of animals Red did not recognize. To the left of the door, hanging on the wall, were numerous tools with odd shapes and sizes. Directly in the center of the room was a watering trough where several more animals were drinking.

As Red continued to scan the area, his eyes stopped abruptly on an unrecognizable animal. The short animal was slightly larger than a pig, with stocky legs and long claws. It was brown with white paws, had a stubby tail, long fluffy ears, and a long, thin snout, like an anteater.

"That's an odd animal," Red thought, as he continued scanning the room.

Several tropical flowering plants and trees were planted in pots and pushed up against the wall next to a small door. Noticing hieroglyphics on the door, Red squinted, trying to see the detail in the dimly-lit room. Frustrated that he was unable see, he realized the only light in the room was coming from the opening in the loft.

"I wonder where Tulio is?" he thought to himself.

As he crawled to the other side of the loft, he headed for the opening that revealed the bright light from outside. As he looked at the city in the light of day, he noticed amazing buildings of all sizes within the city walls. The largest building was directly in the middle of the city. It reminded Red of a Mayan Temple or an Egyptian Pyramid. There were a few smaller buildings scattered on the outskirts. People were hurrying all over the city, but a large concentration of people gathered in a farmers' market in the center of town. As Red noticed the river beyond the city, he could see the suspension bridge where they had suddenly found themselves and had seen the warriors crossing the river the previous night.

A sudden thump sounded behind Red, startling him.

He turned around quickly to see Tulio standing directly behind him.

"Are you the only one awake?" he asked curtly.

"Yes," Red replied, shocked by Tulio's abrupt demeanor.

"What are you doing?" asked Tulio, pointing to the window.

"I was just looking out on the city," Red replied softly.

"Were you seen by anyone?" Tulio questioned.

"No! I haven't been seen by anyone," Red replied defensively.

Tulio took a deep breath, relaxing slightly, and asked, "Did you get a good night's sleep?"

"Yes, I slept well, until I started dreaming," Red replied.

Tulio smiled and said, "I hope you will have the strength you need. Today is going to be a long day. We will be traveling into the city, searching for your friend, and the danger will be very high."

"I will be fine, but why is the danger high?" Red asked nervously.

"As I was in the city this morning, I found that the Gadianton robber's have already spread the word that strangers are among us. I was told that the first man to find the boys wearing strange clothes and carrying odd packs on their backs will be rewarded with great riches," Tulio replied.

"You didn't tell them about us, did you?" Red asked.

"No! Riches are not what I seek," Tulio answered, irritated by the question.

Red grinned and asked, "Then what are we going to do? We won't be able to go to the city to look for Bear dressed like this!" he exclaimed.

"That is why I've brought you some of my clothes and shoes to wear. Hopefully, we will be able to disguise you enough so that no one will realize you don't belong in our city," explained Tulio.

"How long have you been awake?" asked Red, looking down at his watch, sure the time was not correct.

"I've been up since the sun rose this morning," Tulio replied.

"Is that very long?" asked Red, confused by the statement.

"Quite a while," Tulio replied. "There is only a little while before it is time to eat again."

"Lunch already?" squeaked Red. "Wow! I didn't realize it was that late."

"I'm afraid that if we don't get started looking for your friend, the day will end before we've found him, and then another day will have passed with your friend in great danger," said Tulio. "Especially now, with everyone in the city looking for you."

"That is if he's not already captured!" interjected Red, worried about Bear.

"My prayers this morning included his safety. Did yours?" Tulio questioned.

"Yes, of course they will include Bear, when I get around to saying them," Red answered, snickering at Tulio's comment.

"You've not said a prayer of thanks to the Lord yet

today?" Tulio asked, shocked at Red's sarcastic comments. "I thought you said the Lord had sent you on this mission, and you have not acknowledged him by praying?"

"I'd only been up a few minutes before you came up to the loft, Tulio," Red snapped, surprised by his reaction.

"I'm sorry," Tulio replied. "I forget that everyone has a different way of saying their prayers. Nephi told me that I needed to be more tolerant of others. I just don't understand how the Lord can give us so much and we do not recognize or appreciate those things."

"I recognize and appreciate what He has done for me," Red gruffly responded, as he walked to the pile of clothes Tulio had dropped on the floor.

"Are these the clothes I need to wear?" asked Red, trying to change the subject.

He knew that he did not say his prayers like he should, and he was positive that he was not grateful like he should be for all that he had. But he did not like Tulio reminding him of that.

"Yes, in that pile you will find a shirt, skirt or pants, along with the sandals that I brought. When everyone is ready, signal me by throwing a rock downstairs," Tulio instructed. "I must finish a few more chores before we leave, or Captain Gilead will most certainly be angry with me."

"He doesn't seem like a very nice man," said Red, as he looked up at Tulio.

"He's not!" answered Tulio. "He's a bad man! There is no room for love in his heart. You can tell by the way he orders me around. I don't want to ever be like him."

"How did you come to work for him?" asked Red, as he started to change his clothes.

"My father was killed in battle one year ago. I, being his only son, was left to repay his debt to Captain Gilead," Tulio replied.

"What? Why do you have to repay his debt? You didn't make it," said Red. "That seems pretty unfair to me."

"Unfair or not, that is the law. I must keep the laws of the land," Tulio replied.

"Wow! I can't believe that. What about your mom? Is she still alive?" asked Red.

"Yes, she is. She lives in a small cottage just south of the great temple," Tulio replied.

"Do you see her very often?" asked Red.

"No. I'm not allowed to see her until the debt is repaid," answered Tulio.

"You haven't seen your mom for a year, and you can't see her until the debt is repaid?" quizzed Red. "That's terrible! How much longer do you have to work for Captain Gilead before the debt is repaid?"

"I will never be able to repay the debt. I will have to work for him until I die," Tulio replied, as he stared out the opening, across the city.

"What do you mean?" questioned Red.

"I fulfilled my father's obligation a long time ago, but he will not release me. Captain Gilead said that I have not worked hard enough to earn freedom from my father's debt; I have only worked enough to pay him for providing a place to sleep and food to eat. He told me I would never see my mother again," Tulio answered.

"You said that you were in the city earlier today, couldn't you have met your mother quickly while you were out?" asked Red.

"Sneak?" he asked.

"Yeah, sneak," replied Red.

"I've thought about that several times, but Captain Gilead's men are all around the city. If one of them saw me and reported it to him, my mother would lose everything she has—including her home," replied Tulio. "I could not bear to have been the cause of that."

"I'm sorry, Tulio. I can't believe what I'm hearing," said Red

"It is time. We must go. Wake everyone. Have everyone get dressed in the clothes that I brought, and I will get food for us before we leave," requested Tulio, as he climbed down the wobbly, wooden ladder. "Remember to stay quiet and out of sight. I'll return as soon as I can."

"Okay, Tulio. We'll be ready when you return," Red replied, as he watched his new friend disappear out the barn door.

As the door closed, Red turned and quickly hurried to the pile of straw on the floor. He shook Stick's shoulder and said, "Stick, wake up! Wake up! Hurry, we've got to go."

"Leave me alone, Red. I'm tired," replied Stick.

"No, you've gotta get up," insisted Red. "Tulio is going to take us into the city to look for Bear."

Stick's eyes popped opened and he asked, "Tulio?

You mean my dream was real?"

"Yep, we're really in *Book of Mormon* times. Now, get up and get dressed," demanded Red. "You too, Runt. Get up! We've got to go find Bear," said Red, as he shook Runt's shoulder.

"How are we gonna find him?" asked Runt. "We don't know where to look, and we've got nothing to wear."

"Tulio brought us some clothes to wear. He's gonna take us into the city, as soon as we're ready. It's already lunch time. Come on, guys, get up! We've got to get moving today," commanded Red, as he threw the clothes toward Stick. "I bet Bear is scrunched up in a ball, hiding and scared for his life."

Stick and Runt slowly sat up and glanced around at their surroundings. Unsure they were ready to face the day's events, they slowly changed into the clothes from Tulio, while Red told them the story about what he had heard concerning their new friend and Captain Gilead.

"How were we so lucky to find Tulio?" asked Runt, amazed at the guidance they had already received from the Lord. "He's probably the only righteous Nephite in the entire city of Zarahemla!"

"I guess when the Lord asks you to help Him, He provides everything needed to do what He asks," answered Stick.

"I sure hope Bear is all right," said Runt. "I'm really worried. He's a little too young to be alone on a *Book of Mormon* adventure."

"I agree. I wish I'd been the one to get separated. Bear is so young and small, he's got to be frightened," agreed Red.

"Well, let's just hurry. I'm sure he's all right. The longer we sit talking about him being missing, the longer it will be before we find him," said Runt.

As Stick and Runt finished dressing and repacking their backpacks, Tulio climbed back up the ladder carrying a basketful of fruit. As he reached the loft, he set the food on the pile of straw.

"I'm sorry that I don't have more food for you. I was afraid that someone might get suspicious and come looking to see who I'm taking all the food to," he explained.

"This is great, Tulio," squealed Red, as he reached over to grab what he thought was a plum. As he sunk his teeth into the leathery skin of the fruit he tasted the sweet, grainy, texture and started to gag several times. He looked over to Tulio and asked, "What type of fruit is this?"

"I believe you picked up a fig," Tulio replied, smiling at the look on Red's face. "There are plums over here if that is what you were looking for."

Red swallowed hard, forcing the fig down his throat. Then he grinned and said, "Thank you for finding us something to eat. I know it is dangerous for you to have us here."

"No problem," replied Tulio, glad all his efforts were acknowledged. "We've got to get moving if we are to search the entire city as we look for your friend."

"I'm ready," replied Red, as he pulled his backpack on underneath his shirt so that it could not be seen.

Tulio watched as the boys quickly finished off the entire bowl of fruit—everything except the figs. Then the boys hid their clothes underneath the straw, where they were sure they would not be seen. Then Stick and Runt pulled on their backpacks, waiting nervously to find out what Tulio wanted them to do next.

Tulio climbed down the wobbly ladder, opened the door to the barn, and scoured the area for any sign of Captain Gilead's men. Without saying a word, he motioned for the three teammates to follow. As the boys followed Tulio's lead, they were quickly on their way to the streets of Zarahemla. Red watched in awe as they passed several beautiful buildings on their way toward town. He wanted to stop and look at all of the amazing hieroglyphics, but he was afraid of bringing unwanted attention to the group.

As they continued, Stick was overwhelmed by all the birds singing in the forest. Sure he was the foremost expert on birds in the town of Timber Creek, he was excited to hear several birdcalls that he didn't recognize.

Runt carefully checked behind every large rock, tent, and everything else big enough for Bear to hide inside. Softly calling his name every few seconds, he hoped finding Bear would be fairly easy. He just wanted to quickly get through the adventure and get back home.

As the boys walked into the huge, open market, they stayed near each other, but remained far enough apart so that no one would know they were together. That way, no one would suspect that they were the boys that Commander Giddianhi was looking for. As they looked around the market, they found wares of every kind—from clothes and shoes to cooking supplies. The bartering system seemed to be the only way prices were discussed with the merchants, who would accept most any form of payment. Tulio paid little or no attention to the men holding up things for him to buy. He spoke with several men for nearly ten minutes, as the boys continued to wander around the market. Then he motioned for the teammates to follow him.

"I think we might have a lead on your friend," Tulio said excitedly.

"Great! Where is he?" asked Red. "Let's go get him right now."

"I don't think it will be a matter of getting him," replied Tulio. "I think it's going to be a matter of finding and saving him," he said.

Just as Tulio started to turn and head west out of the market, Runt asked, "Hey, isn't that one of the men that was chasing us last night?"

"Yeah, I think you're right, Runt. That is one of the men who chased us last night," agreed Stick, pointing to the man.

"Where is he going?" asked Red. "He looks suspicious."

"I don't know. Should we follow him?" asked Stick.

"No," said Tulio. "It's too dangerous."

"He might lead us to Bear. We've got to follow him," insisted Runt, as he started to cross the street and follow the man.

"Oh, this is not a good idea, guys. If we are caught, we will be killed," warned Tulio.

"We've got to do something. We're not having any luck wandering through the city streets," replied Stick, as he hurried to catch up with Runt.

Red looked at Tulio, shrugged his shoulders and said,

"Come on. We better hurry if we're gonna keep up with them."

The boys followed the man, being careful to stay out of sight. They watched as he suspiciously looked over his shoulder every couple of seconds. He acted very nervous—almost guilty of something. He maneuvered through the city streets, crossing the same street two or three times. Red thought maybe the man was just covering his tracks before he headed toward the hideout. But Tulio was sure the man knew they were following him, and he was leading them into a trap. The man covered the city streets, from one end of town to the other, before he finally stopped in an alleyway between two large buildings. Nervous about poking their heads around the corner to see where the man had gone, Stick had an idea.

"Red, you and Runt walk down the street and pass the alley like you are continuing on down the road. Once you're to the next building, turn around and tell us where he's at," said Stick.

Runt nodded. He nudged Red, and they quickly walked past the alley. As they reached the other side, Runt turned around and mouthed, "He's not there!"

"Are you sure?" Stick asked quietly. "We watched him go down the alley. He has to be there!"

"He's not. No one is," replied Red.

"Tulio, walk with me, quick!" said Stick, pulling Tulio's shirt.

The two boys walked past the alley. They scanned the area, searching for any sign of the man, but he was nowhere to be found.

"Where are we, Tulio?" Stick asked. "How could that guy disappear? The alley is a dead end."

"The building on the right is the meeting place of the high priests, and the building on the left is where Captain Gilead attends his church," Tulio replied.

"Are you sure? This building doesn't look like a church," replied Red.

"Yes, while he attends his services, I tend to his horse and sometimes when I've been bored, I have wandered into this alley waiting for his return," Tulio replied.

"Where does he usually enter?" asked Red. "Here in the alley?"

"No, he enters from the front of the building. But from there I have no idea where he goes," Tulio answered.

"There has to be a secret entrance down there," suggested Stick. "Otherwise, how could the guy have disappeared?"

"I bet you're right, Stick," replied Runt. "We're going to have to find a switch or lever that opens the secret entrance. When we do, we'll find the man that Giddianhi is holding prisoner. Then maybe we can release him and go home."

"What about Bear? We haven't found Bear yet!" said Red.

"If we're lucky he's being held captive with the prisoner," answered Stick.

"I'm gonna walk down the alley and see if I can see anything suspicious," Runt said boldly.

"I don't know how smart that is," replied Tulio. "I will go with you."

Tulio and Runt cautiously started walking down the alley. They studied the surroundings carefully, hoping to find something that would lead them to the opening where Giddianhi's soldier had disappeared. As they reached the end of the alley, they turned around and started to walk back, continuing to search the adobe brick and mortar walls of the building.

As they reached the street, Runt shook his head and said, "I didn't see anything. Did you, Tulio?"

"Nothing, except the hieroglyphics carved into the brick wall," he replied.

"I didn't see them. Where were they?" questioned Runt.

"A little more than half way down the street on the left. They are small and hard to see, but they are there," Tulio replied.

"Should we go back and look? Maybe they're a clue, or they are the instructions on entering the secret tunnels you told us about earlier," Red asked excitedly.

"No, we've got to leave. Right now!" Stick insisted nervously, as he grabbed Red's shirt and started to walk away from the alley.

"What are you doing, Stick?" asked Red, trying to pull his arm free. "Let me go!"

"In a minute, Red. Just be quiet and keep walking," Stick demanded, in a deep, low voice.

"Hold it, boys!" called a man from behind. "Stay right there!" the voice demanded.

"Oh great! Now we're in for it," whispered Stick.

"Don't move. I'll take care of this," said Tulio, as he turned toward the man and answered. "Yes, sir."

"Tulio?" the man called curiously.

"Yes," he replied, in a shaky voice.

"What are you doing here?" asked the man, as he walked closer.

"Captain Gilead, I...I...I...," he replied.

Red knew Tulio was afraid, so he quickly turned around and answered, "I'm sorry, Captain. We asked him to come and play with us for a while. I hope we didn't get him into any trouble."

"I have all my duties completed for the day, and I was just on my way back to the barn for my nightly chores," Tulio explained.

Captain Gilead looked at Red suspiciously and asked, "Who are you, boy? Are you new to our city?"

Red, remembering some of the names that Bubba had told him when they returned answered, "My name is Comonti, sir. I moved here a few years ago from the city of Jershon."

"Jershon? What brought you here from Jershon?" Captain Gilead asked suspiciously.

"I don't know, sir. My father was killed in battle, and my mother moved us here," replied Red, as he shrugged his shoulders.

"Tulio, you have chores. Return home now!" Captain Gilead growled.

"Yes, sir, and my friends?" he asked.

"They can go home as well," he replied, laughing with the men around him. "I don't care about your friends."

"Yes, sir," Tulio replied, as he motioned for the boys to follow.

They all ran as fast as they could, away from the captain and his men.

Chapter Ten

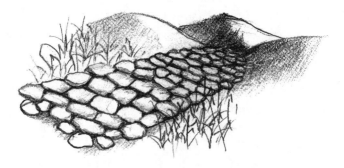

"Wow, that was way too close," said Stick, breathlessly.

"Way too close," agreed Tulio. "It's a good thing Captain Gilead was with a group of men, or we might have been in for trouble."

"You know how to get back to that alley, don't you Tulio?" asked Stick.

"Yes, why?" replied Tulio.

"We've got to figure out where that guy went. If we do, I think we may have found the entrance to the secret tunnels," Stick replied excitedly. "And I don't know why, but I think the tunnels are where Bear is being held."

"We can't go back," insisted Tulio. "I must get back to the barn and get the animals taken care of."

"We have to go back," squeaked Red. "That may be the only way for us to get home."

"Finding those tunnels may have been why we were sent to your time," added Stick. "We've got to go back."

"The risks are too great. Gadianton's men are going to find you here," said Tulio. "We've got to find Nephi. He is the only one who can help you now. We can do that later."

"Is he here in the city?" asked Runt.

"I'm not sure, but I can find out," Tulio replied.

"We don't have a lot of time," said Stick. "We've only been given seven of the Lord's days to solve the problems here. And if we don't, we have to stay in this time forever," said Stick.

"Then I guess we better hurry," said Red. "Tulio, how do we find Nephi?"

"When Nephi is in the city of Zarahemla he always visits a home near my mother's house, located in the southern part of the city. Captain Gilead does not allow me to be in the area, but I can tell you how to find the home," Tulio replied.

"You really can't go with us, Tulio?" asked Runt. "What if he's not there?"

"I will go with you as far as I can. If Nephi is not there, return and we will continue looking for him together," replied Tulio.

"Why don't we just keep looking for Bear instead?" asked Red. "I don't even know what Nephi looks like."

"You've got to tell Nephi what you heard Gilead's

men say," insisted Tulio. "He's got to know that his life is in danger."

"What about Bear's life?" argued Red.

"Red, when we were back in the market, I heard a man saying that one of the boys had been caught and was being held by Giddianhi," replied Tulio.

"Then we've got to go find him. Bear's in serious trouble," Red insisted.

"No. We've got to find Nephi," replied Tulio. "I think he's the only one who is going to be able to help us get Bear Back."

"Tulio's right. We've got to tell Nephi that his life is in danger. That could be the reason why we've been sent here," said Stick.

"And we have to see if he can help us find Bear," added Runt.

"I hadn't thought about that!" replied Red. "But what about Bear's life?"

"I don't think they will hurt him. They're more interested in the prophet and Nephi right now," replied Tulio.

"I sure hope you're right, Tulio," said Red, frustrated with the situation. "I'm never gonna forgive myself for not keeping better track of him, especially if he gets hurt."

"Tulio, you better show us where we need to go," said Runt. "We better get to him before one of Gilead's men do. We need his help."

Tulio started running south through the city on the uneven cobblestone roads. The roads seemed to go on forever as they passed through the city's marketplace, filled with hundreds of vendors selling their various wares. Stick noticed many kinds of food, blankets and clothes. He even saw several strange items that were unfamiliar to him. As Tulio continued to maneuver through the hundreds of shoppers, Runt noticed two of the men that had chased them back in the water system. He immediately looked down at the road, hoping they had not seen him. As the boys worked their way through the city square toward the out-lying areas Tulio stopped abruptly, causing Stick to crash into his back.

"I'm sorry, Tulio," said Stick, rubbing his chin from the collision with Tulio's elbow.

"This is as far as I can go," Tulio said. "If I'm seen any farther than this, my family could be in danger."

"Where do we go from here?' asked Red.

"Continue down this road another few minutes. On the west will be a small barn. Beyond that is a house built from timber, mud and brick. That is my mother's home. If you continue on further east, the next house you will see is a small, run-down hut. The hut is built out of timbers and willows. Nephi usually resides there when he visits Zarahemla," explained Tulio.

"How much longer do we have to travel on these cobblestone roads?" asked Runt, reaching down to rub his aching ankle.

"Not much farther. If you hurry, just a few minutes more," he replied.

"Are you sure you don't want to come with us?" asked Red. "I can't see many people around."

"I would love to, but I can't," he replied.

"Where will you be, Tulio?" asked Stick.

"I'll wait for you here," he replied. "Hurry. You must find him soon. I've got chores to do."

Red, Runt and Stick headed south, searching in an area unfamiliar to them for a man they have never seen before.

"I wonder if Hero had to do this kind of stuff on his adventure?" asked Red.

"I'm sure he did," answered Runt. "Hero got to see a war and people being killed. At least we're not in the middle of a battle."

"No, we're just in the middle of the worst people written about in the *Book of Mormon*. The Gadianton robbers aren't angels you know, Stick," said Red.

"All I'm saying is that there could be worse places we might be," Stick retorted.

"Look, there's a small barn up ahead," said Runt, pointing toward the structure.

"Okay then, let's head east from here for a little bit," said Stick, trying to follow Tulio's directions exactly.

"What do you think Tulio's mother is like?" asked Red.

"We could always stop and meet her," suggested Red.

"I wish that Tulio could see her," said Stick. "I don't understand why Captain Gilead won't allow it."

"I don't know either," said Red. "I'm not sure I could go without seeing my mom for a week, let alone a year."

"Even if I could, I wouldn't want to," added Runt. "There it is—in the trees. That must be his mother's home."

"So, not much further until we reach the home where hopefully Nephi will be," said Stick.

"Nope. I can see it in the distance," replied Runt.

"Do we try to stop at Tulio's home, or do we hurry on and find Nephi?" asked Runt.

"We hurry right now," said Stick. "We can always come back later to speak with his mother."

The teammates hurried toward the hut in the distance. As they reached the quaint home, they noticed that the entire area was overgrown with vines and foliage, which had obviously been left unattended.

"Now I know how all those Mayan cities in South America disappeared," said Red.

"How is that?" asked Stick.

"Just look around here. If this house was left totally unattended for just one year, no one—not even the people who owned it—would be able to find it," replied Red. "The jungle out here is amazing."

"I like how everything is such a pretty shade of green," said Runt. "Back home we're lucky to see anything that resembles the color of green."

"Well, we don't live in the rain forest," said Stick. "We live in the desert."

Standing outside the front door of the hut, Runt asked, "So, Stick, since you're the oldest, are you gonna knock?"

"Actually, I was thinking that because I am the oldest, I would make one of you knock," whispered Stick, as he chuckled quietly.

"I'll do it," replied Runt. "I actually want to meet Nephi. I think that would be way cool."

Red and Stick watched as Runt walked nervously down the small, rock pathway toward the front door. He waited several anxious moments, working up the courage to knock several times on the door. Listening for movement inside, the boys remained completely quiet. Several moments passed without any answer. Again Runt stepped up to the door and knocked loud and hard several times. Again there was no response. The third time, instead of knocking, Runt decided to speak.

"Nephi, are you in there? Tulio sent us."

Finally, he could hear movement inside. The door cracked open just enough so that the figure inside could see outside.

"What do you need, son?" asked a man with a deep voice.

"Nephi, may my friends and I have a word with you?" Runt asked anxiously.

"Why do you think that I am Nephi?" he asked.

"We were told that this is where Nephi stays when he visits the city of Zarahemla," replied Runt.

"For what reason do you need to speak with Nephi?" the man asked, still peering suspiciously around the door.

"Can we please come inside and explain?" questioned Runt.

The man looked out at Runt. He paused only for a moment before opening the door slightly.

"This is not the best place for children to be. Hurry inside, and I, Nephi, will listen to what you have to say."

Runt motioned for Red and Stick to come, and the three walked inside the small, but beautiful, hut. Stick noticed a small, quaint fireplace on the west wall and several chairs that were situated around a beautiful wood table. A small, colorful rug was laid out on the floor. And a few dishes sat neatly stacked near the small sink.

Stick finally looked up at Nephi and was shocked by the size of his chest. He wore a brown, knee-length skirt, a thin, white, linen shirt, and had sandals laced around his feet. His hands were large and rough, and his hair was almost shoulder length. Stick was surprised as Nephi looked at the boys with piercing, dark-blue eyes.

"Are you the children sent by our Father to help find the Prophet Samuel and save him?" Nephi asked bluntly.

"You knew we were coming?" asked Red.

"I thought four of you were coming, not three," he replied.

"We were separated last night while we were being chased by Giddianhi and his men. We have been looking for our friend this morning, but have had no luck yet," answered Stick.

"So, there are four of you?" he asked as he sat down at the table.

"Yes," answered Stick.

He motioned for the boys to take a seat at the table. Then he pointed to a bowl of fruit and asked, "Are you hungry?"

"Yes. Thank you," said Runt as he picked up a banana.

"You've not been able to locate your friend this morning?" Nephi asked.

"No. Tulio said he overheard men in the market say that he'd been caught and was being held by Giddianhi's men," replied Runt.

"Then I must help you to find him," Nephi replied. "And we'd better hurry. I've heard words about a ceremony tonight, and that usually means someone is going to die."

With that, Nephi wasted no time. He lifted his six foot five, two hundred thirty pound body from the chair. Quickly picked up a small satchel, filled it with several things the boys could not see, threw it over his shoulder and then motioned for the boys to quickly follow.

"You must stay with me at all times. Look down at the ground—never into a soldier's eyes. Do nothing to bring attention to yourselves. Our lives depend on your obedience to my words," said Nephi. He opened the door to the hut, peered outside for signs of anyone, and then stepped out onto the porch. "Now, follow me closely."

"Nephi, do you think Giddianhi's men would hurt our friend?" Red asked in a shaky voice, struggling to keep up with Nephi's rapid pace.

"Yes, son. If it served his evil purposes, he would gladly kill your friend," Nephi replied.

"Do you have any idea where to start looking for him?" asked Red.

"The market, I will be able to find the information we need there, but it can also be a very dangerous place," Nephi replied. "We will start there."

"What about Tulio? Are we going to take him with us?" asked Stick, snapping several leaves off as they passed by a tree he didn't recognize.

"You boys are very blessed to have found him. There are very few people who would have taken the risks he has to save your lives," answered Nephi. "Especially since he has so much at stake." Nephi said as he pointed to Tulio's mother's home."I don't understand why he can't see her," said Stick.

"That is Giddianhi's way of controlling both of them. He tells Tulio he will hurt his family, and he tells his mother that he will hurt Tulio," replied Nephi. "Neither one wants to take the risk."

"Can we help them?" asked Red.

"After we save the prophet, I'm hoping to convince them both to leave the city of Zarahemla," Nephi replied. "There are other cities where they will be safe."

The boys walked quietly for several minutes until they reached Tulio.

"I see that you found Nephi," Tulio said smiling.

"Yes, we did," replied Red.

"It is nice to see you again, Tulio," said Nephi.

"It's nice to see you too, Nephi," replied Tulio. "I just wish it was for a different reason."

"So do I, son," Nephi replied, as he placed his hand on Tulio's shoulder. "Now let's go find your friend."

Everyone followed Nephi toward the market, moving quickly to keep up.

Chapter Eleven

As Nephi and the four boys reached the open market, Nephi scanned the area.

"What are you looking for?" asked Stick. "Can I help you?"

"I'm looking for friends that will be able to get the information I need to find your friend," he replied. "Now, do as I said, make no eye contact with anyone."

"Yes, sir," Stick replied.

"Ah, ha," said Nephi, startling the boys. "There he is. Boys, I found who I was looking for. Stay right here. Don't wander off, I will return as quickly as I can."

Nephi turned and disappeared into the crowd of people.

"We have to stay right here the whole time he's gone?" asked Red.

"Yes, and make sure you don't make eye contact with anyone," replied Tulio.

"Why?" asked Runt. "Does it matter?"

"Captain Gilead and his Commander Giddianhi have men loyal to them all over the city. They're not necessarily dressed as soldiers. So, if we don't make eye contact with anyone, we can reduce the risk of being discovered," Tulio explained.

Red nodded and said, "I guess most of the Gadianton robbers were men that carried on normal, everyday lives. Most people didn't even know who they were."

"That's right, Red," replied Stick. "They were a secret band of men that caused harm and death and in most cases without ever being seen."

The boys paced restlessly for nearly thirty minutes, waiting for Nephi to return. They continually glanced around the area hoping to find Bear.

"Where is he?" Runt asked impatiently.

"Have patience, Runt," replied Tulio. "I'm sure he will return quickly."

"Quickly would have been a long time ago," snapped Runt. "I'm too nervous to wait here and do nothing. I'm getting sick to my stomach."

"Come on, Runt. Hang in there. Nephi will be back soon," reassured Stick.

"There's that man—the one that grabbed my leg," said Red, pointing through the busy market. "Can you see him, Stick?"

"You're right. That's Giddianhi!" Stick agreed. "Hey, he's got Bear!"

"Are you sure?" asked Red.

"Yeah, look! He is pulling him through the market by his arm," said Stick as he pointed.

"We better be careful. We don't want him to see us," said Tulio. "Remember, Nephi said not to bring attention to ourselves. So stop pointing at Giddianhi."

"Should we follow him?" asked Red. He watched every move Giddianhi made with Bear as they walked through the market.

"I don't know," answered Stick. "Nephi told us not to do anything without him."

"Should some of us try to find Nephi and let him know what we saw? Then the rest of us could follow Bear," suggested Runt.

"I'm following him! I don't want to let Bear out of my sight," said Red, as he cautiously moved toward Giddianhi.

"Wait, Red. You can't go alone," insisted Stick.

"Well, I'm not staying here without you two," added Runt. "Wait for me."

"Where did he go?" asked Stick. "I can't see him."

"He's right there," Red replied, pointing. "I'm not gonna let him out of my sight."

"We've got to follow him with or without Nephi," said Runt. "Look at Bear's face, he looks like he's scared to death."

"They're on the move. We have to decide now. Are we following Giddianhi or waiting for Nephi to return?" asked Stick.

"Well, I don't know about the rest of you, but I'm following him," replied Red, as he began to maneuver cautiously through the people in the market.

"I don't think we should go without Nephi," insisted Tulio.

"I'm with Red. I can't lose Bear again. I'm the one responsible for him," Stick replied nervously. "I've got to follow Bear with him, I don't want Red or Bear to die."

"You can stay if you want to, Tulio," said Runt. "Maybe you can tell Nephi where we've gone."

Acting like private eyes, the three boys sneaked through the city, secretly following Commander Giddianhi and Bear. They weaved cautiously between buildings, behind plants, trees and people, attempting to stay out of the commander's view, as he walked deeper and deeper into the city. Criss-crossing the street like the other man had done earlier, Giddianhi covered many of the streets of the city, until they finally reached the High Priests' Temple and church building.

"How can I get Bear's attention?" whispered Stick.

"Why?" whispered Runt.

"If he knows that we're following him, then he'll know he can try to get away," replied Stick.

"We could try to throw a rock at him," suggested Red.

"What happens if we hit Giddianhi?" asked Runt.

"Then we all get caught, I guess," Runt whispered shrugging his shoulder and smiling.

"What if we yelled his name?" said Red. "It's not like we're the only people in the area. And I doubt anyone else has the name Bear."

"We could try it," agreed Stick.

"Who wants to yell Bear's name?" asked Runt, nervous they might be caught.

"I will," replied Red.

Without any warning Red suddenly screamed in a high pitch tone, "Beeaarr!"

"You can't yell it like that," laughed Stick. "I couldn't even understand what you were saying."

"I was trying not to get caught," replied Red. "Why don't you try it?"

Stick motioned for Runt and Red to follow him behind the corner of the building. Then he took a deep breath and yelled, "Bear! Bear!"

Giddianhi stopped abruptly. He turned and looked around the area to see if he could see where the yelling came from.

As the boys hid around the corner, they could see Bear smile. They immediately knew he understood that they were close by.

"Why are you smiling, boy?" Giddianhi demanded angrily. "There is nothing to smile about where you're going."

Bear did not respond, so Giddianhi yanked his arm and began walking faster toward the temple. Not wanting to let Giddianhi out of their sight, the boys hurried to stay close.

As they looked around the area, Runt whispered, "This is the same place where that other guy disappeared this morning."

Giddianhi rounded the corner, heading down the

same alleyway. Runt suddenly took off in a dead run. He hoped he could catch a glimpse of where Giddianhi entered the secret tunnels. But, as Runt ran by, both Giddianhi and Bear had disappeared before he could see where they had gone.

"I missed him. He's already gone," Runt said dejectedly. "What should we do?"

"Let's check out those hieroglyphics again. I'm betting they are the key to the tunnels," said Stick.

The boys walked into the alley, straight toward the drawings engraved on the wall.

"I wish Cheri was here to translate the writings for us," said Stick. "That would make finding the entrance a lot easier."

"That would be really nice," agreed Red. "We might know what we're supposed to do for sure."

"Can either of you remember what any of the hieroglyphics meant when we were looking for Moroni's treasure?" asked Stick.

"Not really," replied Red.

"I have an idea," said Stick, as he pulled his backpack off his shoulder and set in on the ground.

"What's the idea, Stick?" asked Red, as he watched him unzip the front pocket.

Stick pulled out a blank piece of paper and a pencil. Then he said, "What if we hold the paper over the hieroglyphics and rub the pencil across the paper so that we can get a perfect image of the picture? Then, when we get back to the barn tonight, we can call Hero, describe it to him and see if Cheri can tell us what it means."

"Great idea, Stick!" said Tulio, startling the boys.

"Whoa, you scared me, Tulio," said Stick, holding his chest with his hand.

"I thought you were going to stay back in the market and tell Nephi where we'd gone," said Red.

"I was," replied Tulio, smiling. "But then I decided that you can't have all the fun!"

"What if Captain Gilead sees you?" asked Runt. "Your family could lose everything."

"I asked the Lord for your help. How grateful would I be that he answered my prayers if I didn't bother to stay with you and help you find the Prophet Samuel?" Tulio asked.

"Well, we are glad you decided to come with us," added Red. "Who knows what we're going to find when we locate the secret tunnel?"

"How do we copy the hieroglyphics?" asked Tulio.

"It's easy! Watch this," replied Stick. He held the paper over the engraved hieroglyphics, turned the pencil tip flat and started rubbing it across the paper.

Tulio watched in awe as the image started to appear on the paper. The image took several minutes to copy. When Stick was done, he pulled the paper away from the bricks to reveal an almost perfect duplicate.

"I can't wait to call Hero back home," Red said excitedly. "I'm sure that Cheri will be able to tell him what all of these hieroglyphics mean."

"Call who?" asked Tulio, confused by Red's comments.

"One of our friends back home," replied Red.

"If you yell into the box, he hears you in another

time?" asked Tulio, with a puzzled look on his face.

"No, no. We have a walkie-talkie. It's a thing that we talk into that sends our voices back to our time so our friend can hear us," explained Red.

"You can't believe how dumb that just sounded, Red," said Stick, smiling.

"You even confused me, Red," said Runt, as he continued to stare at the hieroglyphics.

"Me, too. I don't understand," said Tulio.

"How would you have described what it does, guys?" asked Red, pushing at Stick's shoulder. "Tulio, when we get back to the barn, how about I show you what I mean?" asked Red

"Yes, I think that would be good," Tulio replied, still confused.

"We better get back to the market and let Nephi know what we found," suggested Stick.

"After that, we can get back to the loft so we can call Hero," added Red.

"Stick, before we leave, can I see the paper?" asked Runt.

"Sure," Stick replied, holding out the paper for Runt. "Why?"

"I want to make sure you got a good copy of this thing that looks like one eye staring at you," Runt replied. He took the paper and held it up against the brick wall, just to the side of the hieroglyphics.

"You know, I can usually read or at least decipher hieroglyphics, but I don't understand this drawing at all," said Tulio, looking over Runt's shoulder.

"What's up, Runt? What are you seeing?" asked Stick, comparing the two pictures with Runt.

"Oh, nothing really," he replied. "It's just if you look closely, you can see an eagle with its wings spread open. It has a large jewel on its head and two smaller jewels under its feet. Right below that is a pair of wings that sit on the head of a king. But the king only has one eye open—like he's trying to hide something."

"A king with wings on his head?" questioned Red, as he maneuvered closer to see the drawing.

"Hey, you're right. That does kinda look like a king," agreed Stick. "So, what is the problem?"

"Can you see how the jewels placed by the eagle's head and feet lay flat?" Runt asked.

"Yes," answered Stick.

"Well, look at the eye," Runt said. "The surface is rounded, so wherever you move, it's like the eye is following you," Runt responded, as he scrunched down to demonstrate and then quickly stood back up. "Can you see what I mean?"

"I can," replied Red. "But the eye looks like a button to me—one you push to play a video game, only not as big," he said as he reached up and pushed the eye with his finger.

Suddenly, a small section of cement on the ground, just at the building's edge, quietly slid open. A hidden staircase that led deep underneath the city was mysteriously revealed.

"What just happened?" screeched Red, nervous that he was seeing things.

"You did it!" shrieked Tulio. "You found the entrance to the secret tunnels. We must hurry and get Nephi and show him what you've found."

"We don't have time. This may be our only chance to save Bear," said Runt.

He crouched down on his hands and knees, stuck his head into the opening and tried to see what was below.

"Can you see anyone, Runt?" asked Red.

"No, it's really dark down there," Runt replied.

"Maybe we should go find Nephi and bring him with us," suggested Stick, as he shook his head.

"Well, you do what you want, Stick," answered Runt. "But with or without you, I'm going down there to see if I can find Bear."

Stick pulled his backpack from underneath his shirt, unzipped the front pocket and retrieved a flashlight. Then he looked at the other boys and asked, "Are you coming or not?"

Red looked at Stick with a frightened look on his face and replied, "I gguueess, I'm coming."

"Me too, Stick. I'm coming," said Runt.

"Tulio, you don't have to go with us," said Stick. "You could go find Nephi and tell him what we found."

"No, I'm going with you," Tulio replied. "You three are going to need my help."

"Good, then let's go!" insisted Runt.

Runt, anxious to start looking for his friend, led the way inside the opening, carefully walking down the steep stairs. Tulio was the last to enter the tunnel. As he walked down several stairs, he watched as the opening to the tunnels abruptly started to slide closed.

"Hey look! The opening is sliding closed," squeaked Tulio in a panicked voice. "What should I do?"

"There's nothing we can do," replied Red, pointing to where the opening had been. "It's already closed tight."

"I don't want to be stuck down here forever," said Tulio, as he pushed on the cement that had just sealed the opening.

"Everything's going to be fine, Tulio," reassured Runt. "You won't be stuck down here forever. I'm sure there's another way out."

"You don't understand, Runt. Some of the stories I've heard about the tunnels are that they twist back and forth, split in all sorts of directions and go on forever. It is even said that some of Gadianton's own men have gotten lost and died down here, unable to find their way out," Tulio said in a shaky voice.

"You're forgetting one thing, Tulio," answered Runt.

"What's that?" asked Tulio.

"We have the Lord on our side. All we have to do is ask for help," replied Runt, smiling.

Cautiously, the boys started to maneuver down the winding staircase, at least one hundred feet below the surface of the city. As they finally reached the bottom, Stick turned off his flashlight. The boys moved slowly around the corner and into a tunnel. Then they waited a minute for their eyes to adjust to the darkness.

"We're completely surrounded by cement in this tunnel," whispered Red. "I think this is what a coffin must feel like."

"Other than you can't move in a coffin," Stick replied quietly.

"Look, up ahead, guys," said Tulio, pointing into the distance. "There is a torch on the wall where the tunnel splits into two directions."

"Which way do we need to go?" asked Red.

"We're just going to have to pick a direction," replied Stick. "Cause we really have no idea which way to go."

"Tulio, can you tell where we are underneath the city?" asked Runt.

"Uumm, if I'm not totally turned around after climbing down the spiral staircase, I would guess that the left tunnel would head east underneath the market, and to the right would be west and lead toward the river," Tulio replied.

"Should we try the left tunnel, then?" asked Red.

"Yep, that will probably work," replied Runt. "I bet that these tunnels all have secret entrances into important buildings, like the temple and the palace. That way, if Gadianton's men want to get in and kill someone in the city, they have easy access in and out without being seen."

"You know, that would make a lot of sense, Runt," agreed Stick. "I could never figure out how so many Chief Judges could be murdered without anyone knowing who did it."

"We better talk quietly, Giddianhi walked in here not too long before we did, and he's probably still down here," said Red, apprehensive of his surroundings.

The boys walked in silence for several minutes. Then Red asked, "Can anyone hear that?"

"No, hear what?" asked Runt.

"I can hear water," replied Red. "Listen."

They continued to walk in the dimly-lit tunnel another twenty-five feet. Then it suddenly opened into a large area. As they peered around the corner of the tunnel out into the open area, they could see a small aqua-blue waterfall. The water fell about ten feet into a small pond, then continued running through the center of the room, disappearing directly west into a tunnel.

On the right side of the waterfall stood a large statue of the jeweled eagle just like the one that was carved into the stone outside the hidden opening. On the left was an even larger statue of an eye, rounded and spooky like the one Red had pushed to reveal the tunnel. As the boys continued to look around the area, they noticed dozens of tunnel openings leading in every direction. Green plants and vines completely covered the dirt on the ground, and the vines had begun to crawl up the walls.

"What do you think this room is for?" asked Red. "And why would someone build it underneath the city?"

"Gadianton robbers built this room underneath the city to hold secret meetings," answered Tulio.

"Where do we go from here?" asked Red.

"I don't know," replied Runt. "What do you think, Stick?"

Stick looked out at the area, scratched his head and replied, "I think that each one of these tunnels leads you somewhere in the city. Where you need to go determines which tunnel you need to take."

"If that's right, then which tunnel do we need to take?" asked Red.

"I don't know. That's what we've got to figure out," replied Stick.

"Where is the picture of the hieroglyphics you copied from outside, Stick?" asked Red.

"Runt has it," Stick replied.

"Can I see it for a minute, Runt?" asked Red.

"Sure," replied Runt. He pulled it from his pants pocket and handed it to Red.

"What are you looking for, Red?" asked Tulio.

"Well, I was wondering something," Red paused as he laid the paper on the ground. "Yep, look at this."

"What, did you find?" asked Stick, excited for a clue.

"A map, I think," he replied. "Can you see all the symbols that circle the eagle and the eye?" he asked.

"Yes, so what?" asked Runt.

"I was thinking that each one of these symbols represents what you will find down each of those tunnels," Red replied.

"Nice work, Red. I bet you're right," replied Tulio.

"Now if we just knew what each of those symbols meant," added Runt, "we'd know exactly where to go."

"We're just gonna have to figure it out, Runt," said Stick. "Try to be positive for a minute."

"I can hear someone behind us," said Tulio frantically. "We must find a place to hide."

"Are you sure?" asked Red. "I don't hear anyone."

"Yes, follow me quickly," Tulio insisted, as he rushed into the large open room and hurried to hide in the bushes.

"We have a better chance of getting caught out here in the open, don't we?" asked Runt.

"No, look," answered Tulio, as two men suddenly appeared out of the tunnel the boys had just been standing inside.

The men walked toward the water, laughing and joking with each other. They were completely unaware that the boys were watching them.

"I'm getting tired of taking care of the Lamanite prophet, Ethem," said the man. "Everyday we have to come down into these tunnels to bring him food and water."

"What choice do we have, Morihan?" asked Ethem, as he bent down to collect some water in a pitcher. "Captain Gilead made the order."

"Then why doesn't he take care of him?" asked Morihan.

"I don't know. Are you going to ask him?" asked Ethem, smiling.

"Funny, Ethem. I'm just saying that I'm tired of it. I will be glad when the Captain kills the prophet at the meeting," said Morihan.

"That'll be a ceremony we don't want to miss," replied Ethem, as he lifted the pitcher out of the pond.

"Come on. We've got to check in with Giddianhi before we take this stuff to the so-called prophet," said Morihan.

"I wonder where his God is now?" Ethem asked sarcastically.

Anger stirred in the boys' blood as they listened to the men talk so casually about murder. They watched silently as the men chose another tunnel. Moments later, the men had disappeared into the darkness.

Chapter Twelve

"Did you hear those men?" Red asked angrily.

"Yeah, I can't believe how they talked about murdering the prophet," said Runt, "like it was nothing."

"We've got to figure out where these tunnels go so that we can find Samuel and Bear and save them before the ceremony," said stick.

"Should we try to call home?" asked Red. "Maybe the team can tell us what these symbols mean. That way we won't waste time searching in the wrong tunnel."

"Has the walkie-talkie completely dried out?" asked Runt.

Stick quickly rummaged through the backpack and found the walkie-talkie. "It looks and feels dry. Should I try it?" he asked.

"We might as well," said Runt.

"Here goes nothing," said Stick, smiling nervously. He quickly turned the black knob to ON, and then slowly turned the volume up as high as it would go. Pushing the TALK button Stick called, "Hero, Bubba, is anyone there?" Letting go of the button, he waited for a response.

Nothing happened, so again he pushed the TALK button, and called, "Hero! Bubba! Is anybody there?"

Again, there was no response.

"Do you think the water zapped the batteries?" asked Red.

"I wouldn't think so, but I don't know for sure," Stick replied.

"Maybe it's not completely dry yet," said Red.

"What about the channel? Do you have the walkie-talkie on channel twenty-one?" asked Runt.

"I didn't even check. Let me try that channel," he replied, as he quickly turned to channel twenty-one. As he reached the channel, the static startled him, and he dropped the walkie-talkie into the plants.

"Quick, get it and turn it down. We're gonna get caught if someone hears that thing," warned Tulio.

Holding his hands over his ears, Tulio scanned the area for any sign of Giddianhi's men returning. Stick fumbled through the plants for several seconds before he finally reached the walkie-talkie and turned the volume down.

"Maybe we should try this later when we're in a safer place," suggested Red.

"We don't have time to wait. You heard those men. They're planning to kill Samuel today. And if Bear is with them, then who knows what will happen to him," Runt replied anxiously.

"Runt's right. We've either got to start searching all of the tunnels, or we need to try and get the Team's help one more time," said Stick.

"Well, before you turn the volume back up, did you check to make sure that you were not on a sub-station? Remember, when we use the walkie-talkie for team chatter we don't want Hero's mom to hear, we change the station to twenty-one and cancel the sub-station," said Red.

"That's right! I totally forgot. Good call, Red," said Stick. "Let's try this thing one more time and pray that the team back home can help us."

Stick quickly cancelled sub-station A and slowly turned up the volume.

"Hero, Bubba, can anyone hear me?" he called, nervously anticipating an answer. Several seconds passed with no response, so Stick again called, "Hero, Bubba, is anyone there? Please answer."

Still, they heard no response.

"Do you think we're too far out of range? This walkie-talkie has a hard time sending a signal when we're down in tunnels and stuff," asked Red.

"What is this thing supposed to do?" asked Tulio.

Stick looked up at Tulio and grinned. "I'm sorry, this is called a walkie-talkie. It transfers what you say to another walkie-talkie that is somewhere else. Do you understand?" Stick asked.

Tulio shook his head back and forth and replied, "No, not really."

"Well if we can ever get this thing to work, then you'll understand," replied Stick.

"Try one more time, Stick," prodded Runt. "I don't want to give up yet."

Stick smiled. He nodded his head, turned the black knob louder and called, "Timber Creek Baseball Team! Hero! Bubba! Is anyone there?"

Suddenly the boys heard a tiny voice reply, "Stick, is that you?"

"Yes!" shouted Stick, turning up the volume. "Squeaks is that you?"

"Yep, it sure is!" she proudly answered.

"Where is Hero and everyone?" he asked.

"They're trying to cover for you guys being missing. They went over to your house to mow and edge the lawn. Then I think they're going to your Grandma's house to mow as well," she replied. "They told me to wait here at the Treehouse in case you called."

"I'm so glad you did," replied Stick.

"Is everything okay? Where you are?" she asked nervously.

"Well, we've run into a few problems, but we're working on them right now," replied Stick. "Is everything okay back home?"

"Yeah, so far. Hero and Bubba are trying to keep everything under control. They just wanted me to tell you if you called, what ever the problem is, fix it quick and hurry home," she said, with a smile in her voice.

"We're trying, Squeaks," Stick answered.

"Do you guys need any help?" she asked.

"Actually, we do, Squeaks," Stick replied. "Do you have a paper and pen that you could write something down for me?"

"Yep, what do you need?" she asked.

"I have some Egyptian hieroglyphics, and I need to know what they mean right away. I think Cheri, the librarian, should be able to help. Can you ask her to figure them out and call me back as soon as possible?" questioned Stick.

"Fire away. What are they?" she asked.

"Okay, the first symbol looks like a jelly-fish with only two tentacles—one short and one long. Did you get that?" Stick asked.

"Yep, go on," Squeaks replied. "Hurry, you never know how long we're gonna have a good signal."

"The second symbol is a staff, like the one Joseph used to walk, only with a big, round hook on the end. It has another straight staff with a small flag hanging on the end that crosses it like an X. Do you understand?" asked Stick.

"Joseph, as in the Prince of Egypt?" Squeaks asked.

"Yes," Stick replied.

"Got it. What's next?"

"Okay, the third symbol is a cobra."

"A snake?" Squeaks asked.

"Yes, a snake," Stick replied.

"Okay, next?"

"The fourth symbol looks like the top of a cleaner bottle, only turned on its side," said Stick.

"Do you mean the top handle part with the sprayer?" Squeaks asked, a little confused.

"Yeah, something like that," Stick answered.

"Okay next," asked Squeaks.

"The fifth symbol looks like a pair of tweezers."

"And these pictures are supposed to have meanings?" Squeaks asked.

"Yes, they sure do," Stick replied, smiling.

"Okay."

"The sixth symbol looks like two sticks with a wire strung between them, and there is a necklace hanging from the wire," said Stick.

"Good description. Are there anymore?" she asked.

"Yes, just a few. The seventh symbol is a syringe," said Stick.

"A syringe?" Squeaks asked.

"Like a shot at the doctor's office," replied Stick.

"Oh, okay," said Squeaks.

"The next one looks like a person wearing gloves and boots, lying on the floor," said Stick.

"Okay, that's easy to draw. What's next?" asked Squeaks.

"There are two left. One looks like an eagle with its wings pinned back, and the last one is just a set of wings completely opened. Did you get all of that?" he asked.

As Stick released the TALK button, all the boys could hear was static.

"Oh no, we lost her," squealed Red.

"What are we going to do now?" asked Runt.

"I don't know," snapped Stick.

"Try to call the girl again," suggested Tulio.

Runt smiled and said, "Yeah, Stick, try to call her again."

Stick pushed the TALK button and called, "Squeaks, are you there?"

"Hey, where'd ya go?" she asked. "I thought I lost you!"

Stick took a deep breath and released it quickly. Then he said, "No, we're here. Did you get those last two descriptions of the symbols?"

"Yes, I'll get these to Hero right away. We'll take them to Cheri for help in translating them as quick as possible," she replied.

"Squeaks, we need them right away," Stick said in a serious tone.

"I'll have the information for you in the next hour or two," she replied. "Even if I have to go to Cheri myself."

"Thanks, Squeaks. I'm glad I can count on you!" he replied softly.

"Oh, by the way, Stick, where are you?" she asked.

"We're in *Book of Mormon* times," Stick teased.

"Funny!" she replied. "Where in *Book of Mormon* times are you?

"We're in the time of Samuel the Lamanite," Stick replied.

"Cool. I can't wait to tell everyone. Be careful. I'll talk to you soon. Have your walkie-talkie on in one hour. Over and out," she called.

Stick smiled as he turned off the walkie-talkie. He slowly pushed it inside the pocket of his backpack and zipped the pocket closed.

"Who was…where did that voice come from?" asked Tulio, with a confused expression on his face.

"That was Squeaks. She is a friend from our time," replied Runt.

"Do you think that she will be able to get you the information you need?" asked Tulio.

"I'm sure that she will," replied Red.

"Tell me more about this book that you keep speaking of?" asked Tulio.

"The *Book of Mormon*?" questioned Runt.

"Yes, the *Book of Mormon*," he replied.

"It is a book that was translated with the Lord's help in our time, by a man named Joseph Smith, Jr. Joseph received the Gold Plates from the Lord, which were records written by the prophets of your time about the events and people in your day," Runt explained. He pulled the book from his backpack and handed it to Tulio.

Tulio took the book from Runt's hand and rubbed the uneven texture of the front cover.

"Open it," suggested Red.

Tulio looked up and seemed almost a little frightened of what was inside. Looking back at the small blue book in his hand, he asked, "What is this material? Is this a special skin from the Lord?"

"No, not really," replied Runt. "This is cow hide."

"You have blue cows?" questioned Tulio, with a strange expression on his face.

"No, no. This is a normal cowhide that has been dyed a different color," explained Stick.

"How?" asked Tulio.

"Soaked in crushed flowers to dye the leather," replied Stick, hoping Tulio would understand.

"Oh," Tulio replied, still unsure about the strange book.

"Important information is inside," said Red. He reached out and opened the book in Tulio's hand.

Tulio stared quietly at the pages for several minutes. Then he finally looked up at the boys and said, "I can't read what is written. What language is this?"

"This is written in the language that we speak," replied Stick.

"You speak the same language as I do," replied Tulio, acting even more confused.

"Actually, we speak a language called English," said Red.

"That is not what my language is called. I speak a mix of Hebrew and Egyptian. That is what I've heard you speak—not this language," insisted Tulio, holding out the book toward Stick.

"We speak all of those languages," said Stick, trying to calm Tulio.

"And you read this as well," he asked.

"Yes, would you like me to read you what is says about Samuel the Lamanite?" asked Runt, as he took the book from Tulio's hands.

"Yes, but only if you are sure it is from the Lord," replied Tulio.

"It is, Tulio," replied Runt.

Runt quickly looked up Samuel in the index of the book and found several references to Samuel the Lamanite. "Alright, I'm going to read the beginning of Helaman chapter thirteen, verses one through three.

"Chapter thirteen, 'Samuel the Lamanite prophesies the destruction of the Nephites unless they repent—They and their riches are cursed—They reject and stone the prophets, are encircled about by demons, and seek for happiness in doing iniquity.'

> "Verse one—'And now it came to pass in the eighty and sixth year, the Nephites did still remain in wickedness, yea, in great wickedness, while the Lamanites did observe strictly to keep the commandments of God, according to the law of Moses.'
>
> "Verse two—'And it came to pass that in this year there was one Samuel, a Lamanite, came into the land of Zarahemla, and began to preach unto the people. And it came to pass that he did preach, many days, repentance unto the people, and they did cast him out, and he was about to return to his own land.'"

"You can stop there," Tulio said softly. "I know the things you speak are true."

"How do you know?" asked Red.

"I was one of the people he preached repentance to," Tulio replied. "But many of my people wanted to kill him. They did not want to listen to his words. They didn't want anyone to tell them that they shouldn't do some of the things they were doing. So they chased him away and cast him out of the city. That is when he disappeared a few days ago, and I started to search for him."

"At least you listened to him," said Runt.

"I wanted Samuel to visit my mother and teach her the ways of the Lord. I was hoping she would also believe the things that he taught are true and are the ways of righteousness," Tulio replied.

"Well, there's no need to worry, Tulio. We'll find him, and hopefully he will have a chance to teach your mother," said Red.

"I will pray for that opportunity," he replied.

"What do we do now?" asked Runt. "Should we wait, or should we start exploring the tunnels?

"I think we should wait," answered Stick.

"I think we start searching the tunnels," said Red. "I don't want to sit here wasting time. We really don't have that long."

"The girl said she would get back to you quickly with the information we need to continue our search for Samuel. Our lives will be in less danger if we stay and wait. I don't want to be caught, if that means we cannot save the Prophet," Tulio said.

"We've already waited fifteen minutes, Red. Hopefully Squeaks will have the information soon, and then we can start searching. Okay?" reasoned Runt.

"Alright, let's wait one hour. Then I'm gonna start searching for him," said Red, as he looked at his watch to see the time.

Chapter Thirteen

S queaks, excited to have heard from Stick, turned the walkie-talkie off. She threw it into her backpack and raced out of the Treehouse and down the ladder. Once she reached the bottom, she ran to the front yard. She grabbed the handlebars of her purple bike and threw her backpack into the pink basket on the front. She unbuckled the helmet from her seat, quickly placing it on her head and buckled the straps under her chin. Then she climbed on the bike and raced down the street.

Stick's house was only a few blocks down Fort Street. Squeaks peddled as fast as her legs would move, she reached the house in only a few minutes. She dropped her bike on the sidewalk and ran to the side fence, looking for Hero.

As she peered through the cracks in the fence, she could see that the lawn had already been mowed and edged. She immediately realized that she had no idea where Stick's grandmother lived.

"Oh, great. What am I going to do now?" she wondered, as she walked back toward her bike. "I've got to find Hero, and quick."

As she rounded the side of the house, she was surprised to bump into Stick's mom.

"Oh!" screamed Squeaks, frightened, as she jumped back.

"I'm sorry, Squeaks. I didn't mean to scare you, sweetie," replied Stick's mom.

"I'm not scared. I'm alright," Squeaks replied, trying to calm her rapidly beating heart. "You don't happen to know where the Team is, do you?" Squeaks asked.

"Well, I'm not sure, but it looks like Stick has mowed our yard. So, if he's doing what he was told to do, then he's at his grandmother's house, mowing her yard right now," she replied.

"Where does she live?" asked Squeaks, as she bent over to pick up her bike.

"Why?" asked Stick's mom.

"Well, I'm supposed to give Hero a message. I know that the Team is helping Stick get his chores done so he can keep working on the map," Squeaks replied.

"Oh, Stick has the Team helping him?" she asked, smiling. "No wonder the grass is mowed and edged. Well,

Stick's grandmother lives one block north and two blocks east," she said.

"Thanks," called Squeaks, as she headed north.

As she rounded the corner and started riding the two blocks east, Squeaks could see Bubba edging the front parking strip and Tater mowing the lawn.

"I hope they're almost finished," she thought to herself, as she peddled quickly toward the team.

"Hero, Bubba, Tater, guys! Guess what!?! Guess what!?!" she squealed, peddling the rest of the way down the sidewalk and jumping off her bike as she reached the house.

"What's up, Squeaks?" asked Bubba, as he removed the protective glasses from his head.

"Stick called!" she yelled excitedly.

"Really?" Bubba asked excitedly. "They called?"

"Yeah, and Stick needs our help, fast. I told him we would call him within the next hour, and it's been twenty minutes already!" she exclaimed.

"What's up, Squeaks?" asked Hero, as he walked around the corner of the house.

"They called, Hero. Can you believe it?" she shouted.

"Alright! Was everybody okay?" he asked.

"I think so, but the only person that I talked to was Stick," she replied.

"So, what did he say?" Hero asked excitedly.

"Stick needs our help right now!" she replied nervously.

"What do we need to do?" he asked, as he wiped the sweat from his forehead.

"He described some hieroglyphics and said he needed to know exactly what they meant as quickly as possible," she replied.

"Do you have the descriptions with you?" asked Bubba.

"Yeah, in my backpack," she replied, pointing to the pink basket on her bike.

"Well let's get to the library quick!" Hero shouted.

"I don't want Stick to get into any trouble," said Tater. "How about if Butch and I finish up here first. We're almost done anyway. Then we'll meet you over at the library."

"Are you okay with that?" Hero asked, not wanting to leave the work to his teammates.

"Yeah, we'll meet you as soon as we're finished. Now hurry up and get those hieroglyphics figured out," Tater demanded. "We need to get those guys home!"

Hero, Bubba and Squeaks immediately rode their bikes toward the library. They followed their usual route north on Fort until they reached the library. They climbed off their bikes, chained them up to the bike rack, and hurried inside.

As they entered the library, Cheri was not at her desk. Hero scanned the area and quickly found her reading to a group of kids who were sitting on the floor.

"Oh, great! Not again," Squeaks mumbled under her breath.

"Not what again?" asked Bubba, confused by Squeaks comment.

"Whatever you do, don't try to interrupt her," Squeaks warned.

She walked to where Cheri was reading and sat down on the floor. Hero and Bubba followed Squeak's example, sitting cross-legged on the floor.

"What are you doing?" whispered Bubba.

"Don't interrupt her," replied Squeaks quietly, putting her finger to her lips. "She doesn't like it very much."

"How long do you think she's going to be?" Hero whispered.

"I don't know, but it doesn't look like she has much of the book left," replied Bubba.

The three kids sat quietly for almost six minutes, before Squeaks leaned over to Hero and said, "Maybe we should just go find a book on the meanings of hiero-glyphics."

"Should we?" asked Bubba. "I know when you need help that usually means right now, not later."

"Stick did seem pretty panicked," Squeaks replied quietly.

"Did he happen to mention where they were?" asked Hero.

"Yep, he said that they had traveled to the time of Samuel the Lamanite," replied Squeaks, happy that she had the answer.

"Samuel the Lamanite? Are you sure?" asked Bubba.

"Yes, I am," she replied. "Why?"

"That's a period of time during the *Book of Mormon* when the Nephites are wicked and the Lamanites are right-eous. The Gadianton robbers were growing in strength and number. Things were just kinda bad everywhere," whispered Bubba.

"Serious?" asked Squeaks. "Do you think they're in danger?"

"I'm betting they are in danger," replied Hero. "Especially if Stick needs help with *Book of Mormon* stuff—he's pretty knowledgeable about that."

"What do we do then?" she asked.

Hero shrugged his shoulders, just as Cheri finished the book and closed the cover.

"I'm glad you were here for story time today. Remember that I'll start reading a new book next week. I hope you'll be able to join me again," Cheri said sweetly to the children sitting on the floor.

Hero, Bubba and Squeaks jumped up from their seats and raced over to Cheri.

"Hi, Hero. I see that you and your brother are back from your adventure. That's good. Now tell me, how I can help you?" she asked.

"I have a list of hieroglyphics and we were hoping that you might be able to tell us what they mean," said Hero, holding out the paper that Squeaks had given him.

"Well, let's take a look," she replied. She pulled her glasses from the top of her head and put them on. "Okay, you need to know what a jelly-fish with only two tentacles—one short and one long means, a staff like the one Joseph the Prince of Egypt used to walk—only with a big, round hook on the end, and another straight staff with a small flag hanging on the end that crosses it like an X. Then you have a cobra, a cleaner bottle turned on its side, a pair of tweezers, two sticks with a wire strung between them and a necklace hanging from the wire, a syringe, and a person wearing gloves and boots lying on the floor. The last two are an eagle with its wings pinned back and then a set of wings completely opened. Okay, there are a few that I can tell you and a few that I need to look up," Cheri said.

"Do you want me to write them down?" asked Bubba.

"Yes, unless you think you can remember them all," she replied.

Bubba grabbed pencil and paper from the library counter while Cheri retrieved a book on hieroglyphics and their meanings. Once she located the book, she met the kids at their usual table in back and quickly sat down.

"So tell me, how was your adventure?" she asked curiously.

"Scary," replied Bubba. "I almost got eaten by a jaguar."

"Really?" she asked. "Eaten?"

"Yes. He jumped in the air to attack me, but luckily Lehi shot the jaguar with an arrow," Bubba answered animatedly. "And, I also fell off a cliff."

"How did you survive that?" she asked.

"I grabbed a vine and swung across a ravine," he replied.

"Did anything happen to you, Hero?" she asked nervously.

"No, mostly just Bubba," Hero replied.

"So, why do you need the meanings of these hieroglyphics?" asked Cheri.

"Well, we're just interested in what they mean," Bubba replied evasively.

"Squeaks, is that true?" Cheri asked.

Squeaks looked at Hero and Bubba before responding to Cheri's question. "No, actually Stick, Red, Runt and my cousin, Bear, got into the box with the Liahona hidden inside, and they're on an adventure right now."

"Squeaks," snapped Hero.

"Don't get mad at her. She knows that I won't help you if you're not telling me the truth," scolded Cheri.

"I'm sorry. I'm just nervous. I told them not to touch it," Hero replied.

"When they get back…," started Cheri.

"Don't you mean, if they get back?" interrupted Bubba.

"No, Bubba, I mean when they get back, we need to find a safe place to keep the Liahona until you're old enough to be going on these adventures," Cheri suggested.

"I agree," said Hero. "I'm almost tempted to take the Liahona to Mr. Jensen and let him hold on to it for safe-keeping."

Cheri smiled and said, "Well, your teammates probably need this information quickly, so let's get these symbols figured out."

"Stick described the first symbol as a jelly-fish," said Squeaks, trying to help.

"Right, with one long and one short tentacle," added Cheri. "That symbol's name is Amenta, which means Underworld or Land of the Dead."

"What's the next symbol?" asked Bubba.

"The next symbol Stick described as a staff—like the one the Joseph from Prince of Egypt used to walk. It had a big, round hook on the end, and was crossed by a staff with a small flag hanging on the end," replied Squeaks.

"Alright, that is a Flail and Crook symbol. It means royalty, majesty or dominion," replied Cheri. "The next symbol?"

"The next symbol is a cobra," said Squeaks.

"A cobra, a cobra," mumbled Cheri, as she flipped through the pages of the book. "Okay, the cobra is called Uraeus and is a symbol of Lower Egypt, or the lower part of a city. It was also worn on the crown of royalty as a protection. The Egyptians believed that the cobra could spit fire at approaching enemies."

"Gross!" said Squeaks.

"You're right. It would be weird if you could really coil a snake up, put it on your head, and only have it attack your enemies," joked Hero.

"Can you train a snake to do that?" asked Squeaks.

"No, Squeaks! You can't train a snake to sit on your head," answered Hero, laughing.

"What is the next symbol, Squeaks?" asked Cheri, smiling at the kids' conversation.

"The next symbol is the top of a cleaner bottle that is lying on its side," Squeaks answered.

"That symbols is called the Deshret and also means Lower Egypt, or the lower part of the city," replied Cheri.

"That's funny. Why would there be two different symbols of Lower Egypt?" asked Bubba.

"Maybe one of the symbols represents the lower part of the city and the other symbol represents the ruler's lower subjects," answered Hero.

"That is right," replied Cheri. "However, we do not know which symbol is used for which."

"Bubba, are you getting this?" asked Hero.

"Yep, I got it all," he replied. "What's next? I'm ready."

"The next symbol looks like a pair of tweezers," said Squeaks.

"Tweezers, huh?" asked Cheri, as she searched through the book. "Okay, the tweezers are called Hedjet, and they are a symbol of the crown of Upper Egypt."

"Upper as in the north part of the city, or upper as in the people they thought were upper class?" asked Hero.

"I don't know," answered Cheri, shrugging her shoulders. "Are there any more?"

"Yep," replied Squeaks. "The next symbol description Stick gave is two sticks with a wire strung between them and a necklace hanging from the wire."

"I know that one without even looking it up," said Cheri. "That symbol is called Nebu, and it represents gold."

"Maybe they will bring some back with them," said Bubba. "We could all be rich."

"Yeah right, Bubba," said Hero. "What's next?"

"The next symbol is a syringe, like the one they use to give you a shot at the doctors," explained Squeaks.

"That is the symbol called Sekhem," said Cheri. "It represents people of authority. Any more?"

"Just a few," replied Squeaks. "The next symbol looks like a person wearing gloves and boots, lying on the floor."

"That is not a good symbol. That symbol represents an enemy, or death," Cheri said anxiously. "I hope they're not in trouble."

"Me, too," said Hero.

"Okay, the next symbol looks like an eagle with its

wings pinned back," said Squeaks. "And the last symbol is a set of wings, completely opened."

Cheri flipped through the book, looking for the pictures for several moments. Then she finally said, "Here they are. The pinned eagle is called Rekhyt, and it is often seen below the feet of a ruler, to signify that the people of that area are his subjects. And the last symbol is called the Winged Solar Disk, and it represents the form God takes during battle."

"I wonder why he needs to know these," said Bubba. "Some of these symbols are really odd."

"I don't know for sure, but he seemed almost frantic to get the information," replied Squeaks.

"Is there anything else I can do for you today?" asked Cheri, as she stood up from the table.

"That's everything, Cheri. Thank you," replied Hero. "We appreciate all you do for us!"

"Remember, I'm here whenever you need anything," she replied, as she turned and walked toward the front desk.

"We've got to hurry, guys," insisted Squeaks. "Stick wanted us to call as soon as we could."

"Was he going to wait for us to call?" asked Bubba.

"No, I told him to turn on his walkie-talkie in one hour, and we would call as soon as we could," she replied. She pushed the library door open and walked toward the bike rack.

"How long has it been?" asked Hero.

"A little over an hour," Squeaks replied, as she looked at her watch.

"Do we need to call him before we head back to the Treehouse?" asked Hero. "I know how hard it is to wait for information that you need."

"We probably should," replied Bubba, as he unlocked the chain from his bike and sat on the seat.

"Let's go somewhere private," said Hero.

"How about across the street at the park?" suggested Squeaks, pointing to a small park bench.

"That'll work," said Hero.

With that, the three kids peddled quickly toward the park.

Chapter Fourteen

Once they reached the park, Squeaks retrieved the walkie-talkie from her backpack and handed it to Hero.

Hero took the walkie-talkie, switched on the power and turned the volume as loud as it would go.

"Stick, come in. Stick, are you there?" yelled Hero. "Stick! Runt! Come on, guys. Can you hear me?" Hero called.

He released the TALK button and waited, but heard no response.

"Squeaks, are you sure Stick said he would have his walkie-talkie on in one hour?" asked Bubba.

"Yeah, I'm positive," she replied.

"Try it again, Hero," suggested Bubba.

Hero again called, "Stick, Red, Runt, Bear! Is anyone there? Pick up."

Again he waited impatiently several seconds before he asked, "Squeaks, did you do something to the walkie-talkie?"

"No, it worked fine when I talked to him," she replied. "Maybe I should try to reach him."

Hero tilted his head to the left, then scrunched up his mouth, making a face at Squeaks. He pushed the TALK button and again called, "Hello, guys? Is anyone there?"

Still there was no reply.

Squeaks climbed off her bike and laid it on the ground. Walking over to Hero she held out her hand and said, "Come on. Let me try to call him. Maybe I have the magic touch."

She carefully checked to make sure the walkie-talkie was on channel twenty-one. Then she smiled at Hero as she held down the TALK button and called, "Come in, Stick. Are you there? It's Squeaks, over?"

"Squeaks, is that you?" replied Stick seconds later.

Jokingly, she stuck out her tongue at Hero and replied, "Yep, it's me, Stick. I have the information that you need."

"Were you able to get all of them?" he asked nervously.

"Yes, everything!" she replied.

"Great! Tell me what you've got," he begged.

"Do you have a pencil or something to write them with?" she asked before she started.

"Yes, I do," Stick whispered.

"Okay, the first symbol you described as a jelly-fish, is Amenta which means Underworld or Land of the Dead."

"Got it. What's next?" asked Stick.

"The next symbol is a Flail and Crook. It represents royalty, majesty or dominion," replied Squeaks. "The next symbol you told me was a cobra," said Squeaks. "Cheri said it is called a Uraeus and is a symbol of Lower Egypt, or the lower part of a city. It was also worn on the crown of royalty as protection. The Egyptians believed that the cobra could spit fire at approaching enemies."

"That's weird," said Stick. "But okay, what's next?"

"The next symbol was the one that looked like the head of a cleaner bottle lying on its side," Squeaks replied. "That symbol is called the Deshret, and it also means Lower Egypt, or the lower part of the city."

"Two of them have the same meaning?" asked Stick.

"That is what Cheri said," replied Squeaks. "Hero thought one of the symbols might represent the lower part of the city and the other symbol represents the ruler's lower subjects or something like that."

"We'll have to figure it out," Stick replied.

"Stick, what are all these symbols for?" asked Squeaks.

"The tunnels under Zarahemla are labeled with these symbols. We were hoping that one of them leads to where Bear and the prophet are being held captive."

"What? What happened to Bear?" yelled Squeaks.

"Nothing, he's fine. Or at least he'll be fine, as soon as we find him and free him," Stick replied softly.

"Why are you talking so quietly?" asked Squeaks. "I can barely hear you."

"Because we're hiding in the tunnels under Zarahemla right now!" Stick replied sharply. "And I really don't want to get caught. Now hurry up and finish before I lose the signal."

"Sorry, Stick. The next symbol you said looks like a pair of tweezers," said Squeaks. "Cheri said the tweezers are called Hedjet, and they are a symbol of the crown of Upper Egypt. Cheri wasn't sure if it meant upper, as in the north part of the city, or upper, as in the people they thought were upper class."

"We'll figure it out," replied Stick. "The next symbol should be two sticks with a wire strung between them and a necklace hanging from the wire."

"Cheri knew what that symbol meant without even looking it up. She said it was called Nebu, and it represents gold," said Squeaks. "Bubba was hoping you would bring some back for him."

"Tell him, yeah, right, for me, will you?" Stick asked laughing. "What's next?"

"The next symbol you told me was a syringe used to give you a shot—like you would get from the doctor," answered Squeaks. "Cheri said that symbol is called Sekhem, and it represents people of authority."

"I've got it," replied Stick.

"Are any of these symbols making sense to you?" asked Squeaks.

"Yes, all of them," replied Stick. "The next symbol should be the person wearing gloves and boots, lying on the floor, right?"

"Yep," replied Squeaks. "Cheri said that one is not a

good symbol. It represents the enemy, to die or death."

"Death? Are you sure?" Stick asked worriedly.

"Yes, I'm sure," Squeaks replied.

"Well, I don't think we'll be going down that tunnel," Stick replied, trying to relieve the tension in Squeaks voice. Alright we have two left, right?"

"Yeah, the next to last symbol looks like an eagle with its wings pinned back," said Squeaks.

"Yes, that's right," replied Stick.

"Cheri said the pinned eagle is called Rekhyt, and it is often seen below the feet of a ruler to signify that the people of that area are his subjects," said Squeaks.

"And the last symbol is a set of wings, completely opened. What does that represent?" asked Stick.

"The last symbol is called the Winged Solar Disk, and it represents the form God takes during battle," she replied.

"Thanks, Squeaks. Tell Hero everything will be alright. Don't worry about Bear. We're on our way to save him right now," said Stick. "I don't know when we'll talk again."

"Be careful! Save Bear, and hurry home," she said. "Over and out."

"Over and out, Squeaks," replied Stick, smiling.

"I'm worried," said Bubba. "Bear's been kidnapped?"

"That's what he said, but he said not to worry," replied Squeaks.

"That's more reason to worry," admitted Hero. "Stick doesn't always take stuff seriously."

"Would the Lord have let them go if they couldn't handle the mission?" asked Squeaks.

"I don't think so," replied Bubba. "It's just the combination of Red, Runt, Stick and Bear that has me concerned."

"We better get back to the Treehouse and see what's happening," suggested Bubba.

"Do you think Tater got the rest of the lawn finished?" asked Hero.

"Yeah, knowing Tater, everything is already done," answered Bubba.

The three kids set out toward home and the Treehouse on their bikes. The boys teased Squeaks by peddling as fast as they could, making her struggle to keep up with them.

"Wait for me," she cried. "Quit being mean, or I'm gonna tell Mom."

"If you do, you'll never get to go on another adventure with us," warned Hero.

"Yeah, well neither will you if I tell Mom!" she yelled angrily.

"Hero, knock it off. She's been pretty helpful the last few days," said Bubba. "And she was pretty worried about us while we were gone. Tater said she was the best helper."

"Squeaks was?" asked Hero.

"That's what Tater said," Bubba replied.

"I know. I'm just teasing her," Hero replied. He looked back at the tears streaming down Squeaks' face. "You're right. We better slow down."

Hero and Bubba stopped so that Squeaks could quickly catch up with them. As soon as she did, Hero reached over and patted her on the back.

"Sorry, Squeaks. I was just playing. Don't cry," he said. "Tater and everybody said you've been a great help and I really appreciate all you've done to help while I was gone."

Squeaks wiped the tears from her eyes and replied, "I'm not crying, it's the wind in my face."

Hero smiled and said, "Good. Then let's get home and you can tell everybody what's happening with the four boys."

"Really?" she asked excitedly.

"Yep, you can be in charge," Hero replied.

"All right! Wwaaahhhooo!" she screamed.

"Should we stop and let KP and Bean know what going on?" asked Bubba as the three neared KP's house.

"Probably," replied Hero. "They may have to help cover for Stick, Red, Runt and Bear."

They pulled up in KP's driveway, and Hero jumped off his bike and ran to the front door. He rang the door-bell and waited patiently.

KP finally opened the door and said, "Hey, what's up?"

"Do you have a second to talk?" asked Hero, motioning for KP to come outside and close the door.

"What's the matter Hero?" KP asked, suspicious of the look on Hero's face.

"Is everything okay at your house?" Hero asked.

"Yes," KP replied slowly. "Everything's fine, no one suspects a thing. Why, does someone know something?"

"No," Hero replied. "It's just…"

"Just what?" asked KP. "Tell me already!"

Hero took a deep breath and started, "Well, Red, Runt, Stick and Bear went up to the Treehouse alone."

"Yes," interrupted KP.

"And they got into the box with the Liahona," Hero continued, as he walked toward Bubba and Squeaks in the driveway.

"Did they break it?" asked KP.

"No, they didn't break it. They used it," Hero finished.

"What?" asked KP. "They did what?"

"They messed around with it, I guess. It started flashing again and the next thing I knew my mom was asking what the flash of light was outside," replied Hero. "Well, I knew instantly what it was."

"Are you kidding me?" shrieked KP.

"Those four are on a *Book of Mormon* adventure alone?" asked KP nervously.

"Yep!" Hero replied.

"How are they ever going to make it?" questioned KP. "You've got Stick, who is afraid of bugs, Red and Runt who will play a joke on anybody anywhere, whether it's appropriate or not, and Bear, who's just plain too little to go."

"We raced up to the Treehouse, but it was already too late," replied Hero.

"How long have they been gone?" asked KP.

"Since right after you and Bean left this morning," Hero replied.

"Do we know where they are? Have they tried to reach us yet?" KP asked. "Do they even have a walkie-talkie?"

"I just talked to them a few minutes ago," replied Squeaks.

"Stick said everything was fine but that Bear had been kidnapped." added Hero.

"Oh, this just keeps getting better and better," said KP. "What are we going to do?"

"There's nothing we can do," replied Hero. "But pray and hope that they figure out what is happening, fix it and get home quick," replied Hero.

"Do we know where they are?" asked KP. "Please tell me that they are in a real peaceful time."

"Nope," replied Squeaks. "They're right in the middle of the Gadianton robbers."

"Oh man," replied KP, shaking his head. "I can't believe this."

"Do we have everything covered for them?" KP asked.

"I think so," replied Bubba. "Runt was going to stay at Butch's house for a few days, Bear is staying over at ours, Red's mom said he could do whatever. Stick's mom wanted their lawn mowed and edged and his grandmother's lawn done, too."

"Have we done that?" KP asked.

"Yeah, I think Tater finished up while we went to the library and had Cheri translate the information that Stick needed," replied Bubba.

"Where are you heading now?" asked KP.

"We're gonna head over to Bean's house to let her know what's happening, then we'll go back to the Treehouse and check on Tater and Butch," replied Hero.

"I'm gonna finish up my chores and then I'll meet you guys back at the Treehouse," said KP as he turned toward the front door.

"See ya in a few minutes KP," called Squeaks.

KP waved as he opened the door and walked inside the house, nervous about the trouble his friends traveling in *Book of Mormon* times could experience.

Hero, Bubba and Squeaks headed south down the street toward Bean's house, and this time, Squeaks ran to the door and rang the doorbell.

Bean's mom answered and Squeaks asked, "Hi, I'm Squeaks. Could I talk to Bean for just a minute?"

Bean's mom smiled, then nodded and opened up the screen door, inviting Squeaks inside, while Hero and Bubba watched from the driveway.

"No, no, no. Don't go inside Squeaks," whispered Hero.

"I hope she doesn't say something she shouldn't," said Bubba. "We could get into a lot of trouble."

The two boys waited anxiously in the hot, afternoon sun for nearly fifteen minutes while Squeaks remained inside Bean's house. Finally, she opened the door and came outside, running quickly to meet her brothers.

"What happened in there?" quizzed Hero.

"You didn't say something in front of Bean's mom did you?" asked Bubba.

"One question at a time, boys?" replied Squeaks as

she picked up her bike and climbed on. "Now, what was the first question?"

"Squeaks, you're testing my patience," replied Hero.

"I spoke with Bean privately in her room. No one heard us, I was very careful, and she's going to meet us at the Treehouse in ten minutes," said Squeaks. "Her mom did say to let the team know that she was not going to have a sleep over tonight."

"Whew, nice work Squeaks," said Hero. "I was really nervous for a minute."

"Nice job, Squeaks," agreed Bubba.

Back at home, they dropped their bikes in the front yard, hurried up the ladder to the Treehouse.

"Tater, Butch!" called Hero as he threw open the door. "Are you guy's here?

"Yeah," replied Tater from the couch.

"Did you guy's finish the lawn at Stick's grandmas?" asked Bubba.

"We sure did," replied Butch.

"Did you have any problems?" asked Hero.

"No, after you left, we finished mowing the back yard then hurried back here," replied Butch.

"Was there anything else that needed to be done?" asked Bubba.

"I don't think so," replied Tater in a tired voice. "How did everything go at the library?"

"Fine, Cheri helped us again," replied Bubba.

"Did she have all the information that Stick needed?" asked Butch.

"Everything that he asked for," replied Hero.

"So, did you talk to him already?" asked Butch.

"Yeah, we called him from the park and gave him all the information. Then we stopped by to see KP and Bean so they would know what was going on," replied Hero.

"What do we need to do now?" asked Butch.

"Get some food," replied Tater. "I'm starving!"

"When aren't you starving, Tater?" teased Hero.

"Lot's of times," answered Tater. "Like when I'm asleep, or showering, or when I'm already eating, you know, times like that," Tater joked.

"I think it might be good if we're seen around the house for awhile, maybe if my mom sees us, then if any of your parents call, she can tell them we're all just playing," said Bubba.

"You may be right," replied Hero as he shrugged his shoulders. "But we've got to wait here at least until Bean and KP can catch up with us."

Everyone agreed and waited anxiously for their teammates to show up.

Chapter Fifteen

❝ Where to?" asked Red. "I'm ready to go."

"Well, according to Squeaks, there is a tunnel that leads to the Land of the Dead, a tunnel that leads to Royalty, two that have to do with lower Egypt, one to upper Egypt, one that represents gold, one tunnel that leads to authority, one that represents enemies or death, one for the ruler's subjects, and the last represents the form God takes during battle," finished Stick.

"So, which tunnel should we take?" asked Red.

"I think we take the tunnel that leads toward gold," teased Runt.

"Come on, be serious, Runt," said Red. "We don't have a lot of time before the ceremony."

"I can tell you which tunnel I'm not going to enter," said Stick.

"Which one is that?" asked Runt.

"I bet I can guess," interrupted Red. "The tunnel with the cobra symbol."

"Yes, did you hear that they supposedly spit fire?" Stick asked anxiously.

"We've got to get moving. We've been here too long," insisted Tulio.

"I agree," said Red. "I've already had Bear out of sight longer than I was going to, so would you pick a tunnel already."

"Okay, I think we should take the tunnel with the symbol of the man on the floor. It's the symbol of enemy and death. That's probably where Samuel and Bear are being held," reasoned Stick.

"Where is that tunnel?" asked Red, looking around anxiously.

"It's the tunnel left of the eagle statue," Stick replied, pointing.

The boys carefully climbed out from underneath the overgrown palm fronds and headed toward the tunnel. As they approached the tunnel, they could see large rocks that formed the opening in the shape of an arch. The multi-colored rocks were held together with a strange type of cement. Gray, brown and tan rocks were laid on the ground to form a cobblestone walkway, which lasted approximately the first fifteen feet inside the tunnel. The opening was eight feet wide by nine feet tall, and continued as far as the boys could see. As the walkway ended, they stepped in a soft, sticky, red mud that squished over the top of their sandals and into their toes.

"This feels disgusting," complained Red, as he held up his leg and tried to shake the mud from his shoe.

"I wonder how girls can stand wearing sandals. The straps between my toes have rubbed blisters on the inside of each of them," said Runt.

"What kind of shoes do you wear?" asked Tulio.

"Tennis shoes," replied Red.

"What are tennis shoes?" asked Tulio.

"Shoes that don't tear up your toes," replied Runt.

"I'll show you when we get back to the barn, Tulio. We have ours there," replied Stick, smiling.

Runt led the way as the group pushed farther into the tunnel.

"The tunnel is getting too dark, Stick. I can't see anything," said Red. "Should we use the flashlight?"

"Yes, I have it in my backpack," he replied. "Hold on a minute, and I'll get it."

Stick unzipped the small, front pocket of his backpack, quickly removed the flashlight, and turned it on.

"Hey, there are spiders everywhere," squealed Stick. "There's one on me!" he said as he frantically brushed it from his shirt.

"Don't worry, Stick. If you get anymore on you just keep brushing them off," said Tulio.

"Are they poisonous, Runt?" Stick called nervously.

"I don't think so," Runt replied.

"This is so sick. I could feel the spider's hairy legs," Stick complained.

"Stick, the spider was on your shirt. You couldn't have felt the hairy legs," teased Runt.

"I could feel them when I brushed it off my shirt, Runt!" Stick replied angrily.

"Come on. We've got to keep moving," insisted Tulio, as he pushed past Runt and continued deeper into the tunnel.

The boys struggled to walk through the thick mud as the tunnel weaved back and forth for nearly a mile.

"Do you think we have the right tunnel?" Red finally asked.

"I don't know. We could be wrong," answered Stick.

"We know that Giddianhi took Bear into these tunnels today. With all the spider webs in here, he would have had to crawl in order to miss them," said Red, as he wiped one from his face.

"I can hear something up ahead," said Runt, continuing further into the tunnel. "We've come this far. Let's see where this tunnel ends up."

"We don't have time to explore for fun," protested Stick. "Maybe we should head back."

"Come on, chicken," called Runt. "What if this is the right tunnel, and we give up to soon? Bear's counting on us to find him."

Stick looked at everyone, shrugged his shoulders and said, "I guess he's right."

"We'd better hurry," warned Red, pointing to Runt in the distance. "In another minute, we're not gonna be able to find him either."

"Runt, wait!" called Tulio. "You never know what might be in these tunnels."

The boys rushed to catch up with Runt, yelling several times for him to stop.

"I can't see a thing. Where did he go?" Stick asked nervously.

Barely able to see in front of them, they continued to walk further into the tunnel calling for Runt.

"Man, what if we've lost Runt, too?" Stick mumbled under his breath.

"Stop!" yelled Tulio abruptly. "Can you hear that?" he asked.

"Yeah. What is it, Tulio?" asked Red.

"I don't know," he replied. "It sounds almost like music, but I've never heard this song before."

"If this is music, it's way boring music," added Red.

"Have you noticed that we're not walking in mud anymore?" asked Tulio.

"I just figured that out, Tulio," replied Stick, trying to pick himself up from the ground. "We're walking on slick rocks, and they hurt when you fall," Stick whined, rubbing his backside.

"We're kinda walking on a downhill slope," warned Red. "I'm having a hard time keeping my balance. Try to steady yourselves using the side of the tunnel."

"Runt, where are you?" yelled Red.

"Maybe yelling isn't a good idea, Red," Tulio said quietly. "Maybe he's been caught, and we're slowly walking into a trap."

"Stick, help me, I'm slipping!" yelled Red, as he frantically tried to keep his balance.

Stick and Tulio hurried to grab Red's hand before he

slid down the slippery, wet rocks. As they moved close enough to reach him, they began struggling not to slide down the rocks themselves.

"I can't hold on anymore!" yelled Red, as he quickly disappeared into the darkness.

"Neither can I, Tulio! Save yourself!" called Stick, as he started to slide down the rocks.

Stick screamed at the top of his lungs for nearly twenty seconds before he unexpectedly slid safely to a stop.

"Red, Runt? Are you here?" Stick called.

The sound of the annoying music was all that he could hear.

"Red, Runt?" he called again, as Tulio plowed into the back of him.

"Whoa, careful Tulio," gasped Stick.

"Sorry, I didn't see you," Tulio replied as he stood up and asked, "Any idea where we are?"

"No," Stick replied.

"Any sign of Red or Runt?" Tulio quizzed.

"No!" Stick said again.

"I wish I had a torch," said Tulio.

"Me, too," replied Stick.

Suddenly the boys heard a faint call.

"Did you hear that, Tulio?" Stick asked.

"Yeah, but I can't tell from where," he replied.

"Maybe Tater had another flashlight or even a candle in his backpack," Stick suddenly thought, as he pulled the backpack off his shoulders and rummaged through the contents. "I know I saw a glow stick. Maybe it hasn't been used."

He searched for the green glow stick and found it pressed into the side at the bottom of the pack.

"Keep your fingers crossed, Tulio," said Stick.

He shook the stick vigorously for several moments before he gripped both ends and bent the stick. He immediately heard the snap and saw the soft, green glow fill the surrounding area.

"What is that?" Tulio asked nervously.

"Toys from the future," replied Stick.

"Be careful, Stick," Tulio warned, grabbing Stick's shirt and pulling him back. "Look, a cliff."

Stick, grateful for Tulio's help, quickly stepped away from the edge. Plopping down on his stomach, he looked nervously over the edge for any sign of his friends.

"Do you think they went over the edge?" asked Tulio, as he, too, leaned over and looked with Stick. Then he yelled, "Look! There they are."

"Where? I can't see them," replied Stick.

"Below us, holding onto the palm tree, right there!" he replied, pointing.

"Runt, Red, are you guys okay?" asked Stick.

"Do I look okay?" barked Runt. "I've been hanging here for a long time. Where have you been? I can't hold on much longer. I've already had to let go of the flashlight. I don't have anything else to let go of now except me!"

"Why didn't you answer me when I called?" asked Stick.

"I don't know if you can tell, Stick, but it's about all I can do to hang on. Now help me!" Red screamed, panicked at the situation.

"Where's the rope?" Stick asked frantically.

"Think of something else. The rope is in my back-pack," cried Runt.

"What else can I use?" asked Stick nervously.

"I'm slipping! I'm slipping! Hurry!" yelled Runt, completely terrified. "I don't want to fall into the pit of snakes."

"Snakes?" squealed Stick. "What snakes?"

"Look beneath us, Stick," replied Runt.

As Stick held out the soft, green glow stick, he could suddenly see where the eerie music had been coming from. As he looked around the tunnel floor, he saw literally thousands of snakes everywhere. The entire floor was moving.

"Oh, no. I hate snakes!" Stick screamed. He jumped up from his stomach, checking to make sure there were no snakes around him.

"Stick, help us!" Red yelled again. "I don't want to die here."

"I have an idea," Tulio said suddenly. "Give me the sash you have tied around your waist. Hurry, quickly!"

Stick frantically untied the knot, unwound the sash from his waist and handed it to Tulio. Petrified, Stick watched as Tulio removed his sash, tied the two together and threw the make shift rope over the edge.

"Hold your light over here," demanded Tulio. "Red, Runt, can either of you reach the sash?" he called.

"I think maybe I can," Red replied, using all his remaining strength to reach up for the makeshift rope.

"Don't let me go," he begged, as he took hold with both hands.

Tulio held onto the sash and struggled to pull Red up

over the edge to safety. As Stick watched, unable to move, Tulio struggled for several minutes before he finally saw Red's hand reach up over the rocks.

"Stick, help him," called Tulio.

Stick reached out, grabbed Red's hand and pulled with all his might. Just before Red was able to get his leg over the edge, a small snake slithered out of his shirtsleeve and onto Stick's arm.

Instinctively, Stick released the grip on Red's hand, and shook his hand wildly in the air as he screamed uncontrollably. Tulio, holding Red with all his might, shouted. "Stick, I can't hold him. Help me!"

Stick, realizing what he had done, hurried over to Red and grabbed his hand again.

"What were you thinking, Stick? If the fall didn't kill me, the snakes would have!" Red yelled angrily.

"When you guys quit playing patty cakes up there, would you please consider helping me?" screamed Runt. "I can't hold on forever."

"Sorry! I'm sorry. I just have a hard time with snakes. I hate them," Stick replied, as he finally pulled Red over the edge.

"Red, give me your sash quick," insisted Tulio.

As Red pulled it off, Tulio tied it to the other sashes, making the sash rope longer. Then he quickly threw it over to Runt.

"Can you reach it?" Red asked.

"I almost have it," answered Runt. "Alright, I've got it."

Tulio, Red and Stick pulled until they could see Runt safe on the ledge.

"Are you okay, guys?" asked Tulio.

"I will be after I throw Stick down into the pit of snakes," replied Red, trying to grab his arm.

"I'm sorry!" Stick replied. "I didn't mean it."

"Stick, when we get back, we've really got to work on your fear of snakes," suggested Runt. "It's not healthy."

"Well, that was a lot of fun!" Red said sarcastically, as he sat down, trembling. "But, please remind me never to do that again."

"I can still feel their slimy bodies all over me," complained Runt, as he tried to rub the gooey, wet feeling off his arms. "I guess we know this is the wrong tunnel."

"I wonder what fun things we're going to find in the next tunnel?" asked Red.

"Don't say that, Red," said Stick. "It's bad luck!"

"Do you know how lucky we are that no one was hurt?" asked Runt. "Most of the snakes we saw back there were poisonous."

"Oh, great! I had a poisonous snake on me?" asked Stick, panicking again.

"Yeah, are you alright, Stick?" asked Red. "You were squealing like a girl," he joked, pushing Stick's shoulder.

"I was not," replied Stick. "What about you? I think you screamed the loudest."

"Oh, no. That scream belonged to the fraidy cat in the group," Red replied, pointing toward Stick.

"I'm not afraid," insisted Stick.

"What? Yes you are," replied Runt. "In fact, I'm surprised you didn't have a heart attack and have to be recessitated right there on the spot," said Runt, smiling. "For several seconds, you didn't even move."

"I wasn't afraid," Stick protested. "I was completely petrified."

The boys laughed and teased each other, mostly to relieve the tension from almost falling into a pit of snakes. But Tulio knew they had to figure out how to get back to the tunnel above them.

"We've got to get going," insisted Tulio, as he started trying to maneuver his way up the slippery rocks.

"Why don't we take this tunnel back?" suggested Runt, pointing to a tunnel behind the slippery rockslide.

"We don't know where it goes," said Stick. "How will we get back to where we started?"

"What's it going to hurt to try?" asked Red. "I don't think there's any way we're going to make it back the way we came."

"He's right, Stick," said Runt. "We might as well try this tunnel, because we're never gonna make it back up there," Runt said, pointing above his head.

"I don't want to get lost in here either," said Tulio. "Remember, I told you about the stories of men who have died in here because they got lost."

"Well, that's not going to be us," insisted Stick. "We're here on a mission, and we're gonna be just fine. Come on, follow me. Let's check out this other tunnel. Hopefully, we can find our way back."

The boys cautiously set out through the tunnel, following Stick as he led the way with the soft light of the glow stick. Unlike the first tunnel, the boys now walked easily on the dry, dirt floor. There were passageways breaking off the main tunnel, leading in every direction. Unsure where to go, they remained in the main tunnel, hoping it would take them back to the main room with all the tunnels.

Thankfully, almost an hour later, after wandering back and forth through the mysterious, bug-infested tunnel, they could see the end in the distance.

"Look! The rock archway!" Stick called excitedly.

"Ssshhh," insisted Runt, as he covered Stick's mouth. "There are men at the entrance."

"Hurry and put the glow stick in my backpack," whispered Red. He grabbed it from Stick and hid it underneath his shirt, quickly trying to conceal the light, until he could put it in his backpack.

"What are we gonna do?" whispered Tulio.

"Wait a minute. Let's see if we can hear what they are saying," replied Stick.

The boys watched and listened, but were unable to hear what the men were saying. Several minutes passed before the men finally walked away.

Chapter Sixteen

 "I'm gonna go look and see if I can tell where they've gone," said Runt, as he moved cautiously toward the entrance of the tunnel.

As he reached the entrance, and looked out in the open room, he was surprised to see several men standing around. He motioned for Stick, Red and Tulio to come up to the front of the tunnel.

"Can you believe that all of these men are here?" whispered Runt, as the boys caught up with him.

"Are they all Gadianton robbers?" asked Red.

"They may not all be robbers, but they are all loyal to the Gadianton robbers," replied Tulio. "Or I can guarantee that they wouldn't be here."

"What do we do?" asked Red. "Where do we look now?"

"I was thinking we should check the tunnel that is marked with the jelly-fish. Squeaks said it was called Amenta, which means the Underworld or Land of the Dead," said Stick.

"Why do you keep picking all the tunnels that have something to do with death?" asked Tulio.

"I thought that a tunnel with a reference to death would most likely be where the bad guys would hold Bear and Samuel. We overheard some of the men say that they were going to kill them," Stick replied.

"I guess that's good reasoning, but I can't help but think we're just putting ourselves in more danger," replied Tulio.

"I think Stick could be right," replied Runt. "It only makes sense that they are being held in a tunnel marked with death."

"Where is the tunnel that you're talking about, Stick?" asked Red.

"Where are we now?" asked Stick. "We didn't come back from the same tunnel we started in."

"Okay, I can see the eagle statue up on the left, so I would guess that we're about three or four tunnels from where we started," replied Runt, as he carefully peered around the rock archway, being careful not to be seen.

"Then we only have to move one or two tunnels to the right," replied Stick, as he looked at the paper.

"That should be fairly easy," said Tulio. "The plants are pretty thick along the stream. Let's just try to crawl behind them," he suggested.

"You lead the way, Tulio," said Red.

Tulio crawled to the edge of the tunnel, and then quickly slipped behind several large palm fronds. When he was safely hidden, he motioned for Red to follow. One by one, the boys inched their way toward the next tunnel. As they reached the first tunnel, Tulio looked back at Stick, pointed to the tunnel and then shrugged his shoulders. Stick checked the map, shook his head and pointed west, toward the next tunnel.

Tulio turned and continued to move slowly toward the next tunnel.

Suddenly, standing next to the trees and shrubs where the boys were hiding, stood Ethem, Shiz, Lib and Morihan. Tulio quickly motioned for everyone to be quiet and hold still.

"When will the ceremony begin?" asked Ethem.

"Not for several more hours," replied Shiz. "Giddianhi will wait until well after dark."

"What about Captain Gilead?" asked Lib. "Is he coming tonight?"

"Yes. He wouldn't miss seeing Samuel, the Lamanite Prophet or King Tubaloth's child spy being killed," replied Morihan.

"Has the word been spread to the members in the city?" asked Shiz.

"Yes," replied Morihan.

"What about Nephi? Is he here? If he is, who is watching him?" asked Ethem.

"He showed his face in the open market this morning for the first time," replied Shiz.

"How do you know?" asked Ethem.

"His trusted friend, Morihan here, told me so," replied Shiz.

"You're the one he trusts?" asked Ethem.

"Yes, we've been friends since we were children," Morihan replied.

"And he has no idea that you have joined with Gadianton?" asked Ethem.

"No, he would never suspect me. Never!" replied Morihan.

"Everything is working just the way we've planned," chuckled Shiz. "The way of the Lord—who needs it?" he laughed. He slapped Morihan on the back and walked off with the other men.

"I really hate those men," whispered Stick.

"Me, too," agreed Runt.

"He must be the friend Nephi found in the market this morning," said Tulio.

"Can you imagine where we'd be right now if we'd been waiting there when Nephi and that guy returned?" asked Red.

"We'd be in prison with the prophet and Bear," replied Runt. "Now let's get moving and find them before they are killed at the ceremony tonight!"

Tulio led the way through the plants to the next tunnel. Making sure no one was watching, they hurried through the rock archway into the tunnel and ran into the darkness.

As they moved deeper into the tunnel, Runt said, "Red, get that glow stick out of your backpack so we can see what's coming up ahead."

"Yeah, and no running off this time," warned Stick. "I'm not very good at saving you, especially if snakes are involved."

"Snakes? Don't you mean bugs of any kind?" teased Runt.

"Ha, ha! Go ahead make fun—I can take your jokes. Make fun of the guy that hates bugs," replied Stick, as he pushed forward in the tunnel.

"Oh, come on, Stick. We're just teasing you," said Red.

"Hey, look at this," said Tulio, startling the boys.

"What is it?" asked Runt.

"I don't know," replied Tulio.

"It kinda looks like rabbit pellets," replied Red.

"Pellets?" asked Tulio. "What are pellets?"

"Uumm," replied Red smiling. "Like when they go to the bathroom."

"Oh, you mean…," replied Tulio.

"Yep, that's what I mean," replied Red, smiling.

"No. Do you know what that looks like?" asked Stick. "That looks like bat dung."

"Bat dung?" asked Runt. "Where have you seen bat dung?"

"Back in the tunnel with Lehonti, remember?" Stick replied. "We walked all over it."

"Oh yeah, I forgot. Do you think that means there are bats in this tunnel?" asked Runt.

"Oh, I sure hope not," Stick nervously replied, as he held the glow stick toward the top of the tunnel.

"We better hurry. I'm not sure this is any of those things you speak of," replied Tulio.

"Then what are they?" asked Red, as he kicked at the round, black balls.

"No, don't do that!" Tulio yelled, as he watched several of the balls fly across the floor.

"Why?" asked Red. "It's not like a little bat dung is going to hurt us."

"No, it won't, but the scarabs might," he replied, pointing to the thousand of beetles scampering all over the floor. "Run!" he screamed.

Tulio took off like lightning. He was quickly followed by Red, Runt and Stick. All of the boys were screaming at the top of their lungs in fear.

"Do they fly?" yelled Red.

"No, the bats fly," replied Tulio. "Scarabs live near bats."

Frightened by the noise of the screaming boys, the bats dropped from the ceiling of the tunnel and swooped around the boys' heads. Equally stirred up, the beetles crawled and scurried all around the boys' feet and legs.

Runt knew the bats and beetles were following the sound of their voices, but none of the boys could stop their screaming.

"There is a small pond and waterfall ahead," called Tulio.

"Any plants?" asked Runt, swatting frantically at the bats and beetles around him.

"A few," Tulio replied.

"Try to find a place to hide," he called.

Hurrying to the small opening in the tunnel, the boys ran toward the water.

"Hold still. Everyone be quiet!" shouted Runt. "They

will stop following us if they can't hear us."

"They're everywhere. I can't stop," insisted Stick, still flailing his arms wildly above his head.

"Try, Stick," said Tulio. "Try."

Horrified by the bugs all around him, Stick ducked under a small shrub, closed his eyes and tried to imagine he was back in the Treehouse. Occasionally feeling something tickle his foot, he whimpered in fear, but he remained completely still.

Several tense minutes passed before Runt finally said, "Its okay, Stick. You can open your eyes now."

Stick opened his eyes to see a small waterfall spilling into a pond.

"Are they gone?" he asked nervously.

"They're not gone, but they're no longer bugging us," Runt replied. "Just don't move quickly or scream, and we'll be fine."

"What is a scarab, Tulio?" asked Runt.

"It's a beetle," Tulio replied. "Actually a scarab is a dung beetle."

"So, that stuff Red kicked was really bat dung?" asked Stick.

"Yep, the beetles roll it around for some reason, so everyone calls them dung beetles," explained Tulio.

"Can they hurt you?" asked Stick.

"They could bite you I guess, but I've never been hurt by one," Tulio replied.

"I'm gonna put my feet in the water for a minute," said Red, as he walked toward the edge of the pond. I can't stand this dried, red mud any longer."

"Me, too," replied Stick, as he swatted a beetle off his pant leg.

The two boys walked over to the pond's edge, untied their sandals and slipped their feet into the warm water.

"This is the only relaxing thing that has happened all day," commented Stick.

"Are we ever going to find Bear?" asked Red quietly.

"Yes, we'll find him," Stick replied confidently.

"Do you think there's anything in this water that might hurt us?" asked Red.

"I doubt it. It's a pond," replied Stick. "But if you're nervous, ask Runt."

"Runt?" Red called softly.

"Yeah," he answered, as he walked to the edge of the pond. "What's up?"

"Are there scary things that live in the water down here?" Red asked.

"I don't know. Why?" asked Runt.

"I was just wondering if I could jump into the water," Red asked.

"I don't see why not. But we don't have a lot of time," said Runt.

"Maybe just a quick dip," said Red.

"I guess you could, if you hurry," Runt responded, splashing water at Red's face.

"Does anyone wanna go in with me?" Red asked.

"Go where?" asked Tulio as he walked toward the pond.

"Go swimming for a minute," said Red, as he backed up to get a running leap into the water.

Tulio looked into the beautiful water. Noticing something, he quickly reached out and caught Red in mid-air, then carefully set him back on the side of the pond.

"Stick, get your feet out of the water, right now!" Tulio demanded.

"What's the matter with you?" Red asked, with a scowl on his face. "Why did you stop me?"

"Why can't I have my feet in here?" added Stick.

"Both of you, look at the bottoms of your feet. Do you see any marks?" Tulio asked nervously.

Stick lifted his feet and looked at the bottom. Shocked at what he saw, he yelled, "My feet are bleeding!"

"Mine, too!" screamed Red. "What's the matter? What's wrong with this water?"

"Nothing's wrong with the water," replied Tulio. "It's what's in the water," he said.

"What's in the water?" cried Stick. "I can't see anything!"

"Those are piranha," answered Runt. "Right, Tulio?"

"Yes," Tulio replied. "You're lucky they didn't take your whole foot off."

"I didn't feel them biting me," whimpered Red, as he crawled to his backpack and searched for the first aid kit.

"It felt like bubbles coming up from the bottom of the pond, right?" asked Tulio.

"Yes, it felt good," answered Red.

"That was the piranha chewing the skin off the bottom of your feet," Tulio answered.

"How did you know they were in there?" asked Runt.

"I saw them," he answered. "The water is clear, and if you look, you can see their sharp teeth everywhere."

"Why didn't they just bite us?" asked Red. "I heard that they can eat an entire cow in just a few minutes."

"You're very lucky," Tulio answered.

"Either that, or very blessed," added Runt.

Red and Stick pulled gauze from the first aid kit and wiped the blood off the bottom of their feet.

"What now, Stick?" asked Red.

"Do you have some medicated ointment in there?" asked Stick.

"Yeah, with added pain relief in it," Red replied.

"Good, we're going to need it," Stick said. He squeezed a long, round blob of ointment into his hand and started rubbing it onto his feet.

"Should we use bandaids, or what?" asked Red.

"No, let's wrap our feet with the gauze," Stick replied. "I don't know how I'm gonna walk now."

"How do you think piranha got into this tiny pond, Tulio?" asked Runt.

"I bet someone purposely brought them and put them in there," he replied. "The closest lake I've seen piranha in is a half-day's walk from here."

"Why would someone do that?" asked Runt.

"Your guess is as good as mine," he replied. "Maybe Gadianton's men put them here to torture people."

"No! Really? Do you think so?" asked Stick, with a look of horror on his face. "Is that how his men torture people?"

"One of the ways, I bet," replied Tulio.

"Oh, that makes me sick," said Runt. "You know, when I read about these men in the *Book of Mormon*, I didn't really understand how horrible they were. I mean, I knew they were bad, but I didn't know how bad, until now."

"These are very bad men," Tulio agreed.

"I can't believe that one of Nephi's trusted friends turned on him," said Stick. "I would have thought with a friend like Nephi, you could never be bad."

"You never know how enticing money and riches can be," replied Tulio.

"Are you two fixed up enough that you can start walking?" asked Runt.

"Yes, but I'm not going back the way we came," insisted Red. "Hopefully there's another way out."

"Look, behind the waterfall," said Tulio.

"Another opening," Red replied excitedly. "Let's try it."

"You never know where we might end up or what else is in there," added Runt.

"I know, but I don't care. I'm with Red. I don't want to go back the way we came," said Stick. "I don't care to see anymore of those scarab things or bats either."

"Can you walk?" asked Runt.

"I think so," replied Stick, as he laced up his sandals.

"Can you, Red?" asked Tulio.

"Yeah, I think I can," he replied, as he carefully stood up. "I feel okay. I can do it."

"Tulio, will you lead the way?" asked Runt, as he held out the glow stick for him to take.

Tulio nodded, took the stick and headed into the darkness. The path was dry and easy to walk on. It meandered back and forth and was not nearly as long as the last tunnel. The group traveled about thirty minutes before they could see light in the distance.

"I wonder what tunnel we're in now?" asked Runt.

"Let's find out," suggested Tulio.

"First, let's, put the glow stick in Red's backpack," said Stick. "I don't want anyone to see us."

Red unzipped his pack and held it open so Tulio could drop the glow stick inside, then quickly zipped it shut.

"Tulio, do you want to go look and see which tunnel we're in?" asked Stick.

"Sure," he replied, as he started sneaking toward the rock archway.

The boys watched Tulio carefully move into the shadows of the tunnel, as several men passed by. Slowly, he inched his way outside the tunnel, into the cover of the plants and trees.

"Why is he going all the way outside the tunnel?" asked Red.

"I don't know," answered Stick, as he struggled to see what Tulio was doing.

"Maybe he can't see where we are," suggested Runt.

The boys watched for several long minutes before Tulio finally moved back inside the tunnel. He quickly crossed the twenty-five feet to where the boys were waiting.

"We're four tunnels further west than when we started," said Tulio.

"Why did you go all the way outside the tunnel?" asked Red.

"I thought I saw men tied up out there. But, when I moved closer, I could see the men playing some sort of game," replied Tulio.

"So, where to from here?" asked Runt. "Any idea which tunnel we should try next?"

Chapter Seventeen

Stick shook his head, scrunched up his nose and said, "I don't know if I dare help pick another tunnel. I haven't had very good luck choosing one so far."

"I don't think I can handle another tunnel filled with creepy, crawly things," added Tulio. "I don't care much for them either."

"Well then, I guess I better pick the next one," said Red, grinning. "Let me see, how does Hero's little sister Squeaks do this—eenie, meenie, miney, mo?"

"Funny, Red," said Runt.

Runt pulled out the map to look at the rest of the tunnels, accidentally tearing the paper in half.

"Come on, guys. Quit messing around. Now look what you did. We need that paper," scolded Stick, as he picked up both pieces and held them together.

"Stick, can you see that?" asked Tulio.

"See what?" asked Stick. "I only see two torn pieces of paper."

"The paper—you're holding it upside down," said Tulio, pointing.

"Oh, sorry," replied Stick, as he placed the torn sides together.

"No, put them back the way they were," Tulio insisted.

Stick, unsure what Tulio wanted to show him, placed the torn pieces of paper backwards again. "Like this?" he asked, confused.

"Yes, look. When you hold the two pieces backwards, there is a funny looking head, with wings and one eye, sitting on the eagle."

"Yeah, I don't get it, Tulio. What does that mean?" asked Red.

"Look, guys," said Tulio, pointing to the torn paper. "Look at the top of the head."

"The eagle wings?" questioned Runt.

"Yeah, the wings. Don't they represent the form that God takes during battle?" Tulio asked.

"Yeah, that's what Squeaks said," replied Stick.

"Well, don't you think it seems kinda funny that the wings are sitting on top of a mysterious head?" he asked.

"I'm not getting it, Tulio. Where are you going with this?" asked Runt, completely confused.

"Alright, I think the wings on top of the head represent where they are hiding the prophet. We would normally never pick that tunnel because it has nothing to do with prisoners or dying. But when you move the head to the top of the paper, the symbol changes it's meaning to secrecy. It is the form Gilead's men are using. They are planning to make the city of Zarahemla subject to their rule. So, the safest place to hide the only man who could possibly stop or slow them from attaining their desires, is in the tunnel marked by the form that God takes when he prepares to go to battle," said Tulio. "Do you understand?"

"Kind of," replied Runt. "The winged eagle represents the ruler's subjects, the head with one eye open represents secrecy and deceit, and the wings on top of the head represent the form that Gilead's men are taking, because they consider themselves to be as Gods. Am I right?" Runt asked.

"Exactly right," replied Tulio.

"So, do you think we need to go down the tunnel marked on this map with the wings?" asked Stick. "We don't have time for more mistakes."

"I know we don't, but I think I'm right," Tulio replied. "You know, I have a lot at stake here, too. I'm sure Captain Gilead is ready to kill me. I haven't tended to any of my chores today, and I might have put my family in jeopardy as well."

"He's right, Stick," replied Runt.

"We've already made two mistakes, Stick," added Red. "I think he might be on to something here. Let's check out the tunnel."

"All right, I guess. What do we have to lose?" replied Stick, obviously exasperated. "Except time, and our lives?"

"Come on. Knock it off, Stick," said Red. "You can't pick every tunnel."

"Do we all agree with Tulio?" asked Stick.

"I do," replied Red.

"And so do I," added Runt. "You know I like snakes and stuff, but even I've had enough of the creepy, crawly things."

Scanning the map for the entrance to the tunnel, Stick located it four tunnels west of their current location—directly to the right of the statue.

"There are men everywhere," said Runt. "Tulio, do you want to lead the way again? You did a great job the last time."

"Sure," replied Tulio.

Tulio quickly took the lead, heading to the entrance of the tunnel. He scanned the area, noting the location of all the men and crawled quickly into the bushes just outside the tunnel. When he was positive no one was looking, he motioned for the others to follow. Once they were all safely under the cover of some thick bushes and vines, Tulio started to inch his way toward the next tunnel.

As they made their way closer and closer, the boys had to stop several times as Gadianton's men wandered in and out of the surrounding tunnels.

"They're everywhere, Stick," said Red, anxious to get out of the area.

"I can see that," he replied.

"I never thought there were this many men involved," said Tulio. "I'm not sure anyone in the city can be trusted."

"Now you know why Nephi hides in that little cottage outside of town," said Stick.

"I feel bad when I think about how sad he's going to

be when he finds out about his friend," whispered Runt.

"I am, too," replied Tulio.

Finally, they reached the tunnel opening. Red was sure he could hear voices inside.

"Does that sound like Bear?" Red asked excitedly.

"I can't hear anything," replied Runt.

"I thought I heard voices," replied Red. "Listen."

"Before we go inside the tunnel, we better make sure that Gilead's men are not in there," suggested Stick.

"How do we do that?" asked Runt.

Stick shrugged his shoulders and answered, "I don't know. I guess we're just gonna have to be on guard and be really careful."

"There are probably guards posted to watch the prisoners," said Tulio.

"Well, let's go. I want to get this over with," said Red, moving toward the opening of the tunnel.

"Hold it!" said Tulio. He grabbed Red's arm and pulled him back into the plants.

"What's the matter with you?" demanded Red, as he tried to regain his balance.

"Look! Captain Gilead just walked in the main area," said Tulio.

"Oh, man. That means we don't have a lot of time left," Runt said nervously. "We may have to crawl along the edge of the tunnel in the darkness, and find them right now."

Tulio peered cautiously around the entryway into the tunnel. Not seeing anyone, he quickly motioned for the others to follow.

"Okay, here we go," whispered Stick, as he hurried to

follow Tulio. "Pray we're in the right tunnel."

"And that there are no creepy things," added Red.

The boys crawled cautiously in the dark for nearly ten minutes. They struggled to stay in the main tunnel because side tunnels split off about every twenty feet. The boys calculated that they had crawled on their hands and knees approximately one-half mile. Suddenly the dirt floor of the tunnel became a sticky, gooey, muddy mess.

"Oh, this is nice," Red said sarcastically. "Now not only do I have mud between my toes, now I have it between my fingers as well."

As they continued to crawl, a sudden blast of cold caused the boys to shudder.

"Did you feel that?" asked Runt.

"I did. That was weird," whispered Tulio.

"Where would a cold wind come from?" asked Red.

"I don't know, and I don't care. It felt nice for a second, but we need to keep moving. We don't have a lot of time," warned Stick, as he continued crawling deeper and deeper into the tunnel.

"How much time do you think we have, Stick?" asked Runt.

"I'm not sure, but not long," he replied. "I'm sure Captain Gilead will get up and give a long speech. Then maybe he will deal with the prophet."

"This is so not funny. I can't believe this is happening," whined Runt. "I just want to go home."

"Well, if you want that to happen, you better hurry up and help save the prophet so we can get out of here," Stick replied.

"I wish I could go home with you," Tulio said softly.

"No you don't. What about your mom and family?" asked Stick.

"I don't ever get to see them," Tulio replied.

"Well, maybe once we save the prophet, he can take you and your family to another city," said Runt.

"We would love to take you back with us," added Red. "But I don't know if we can."

"I understand," Tulio replied sadly.

"Ssshhh," whispered Stick. "I hear something. Everybody listen."

"I hear it, too," replied Runt. "There are voices up ahead."

"What do we do?" Red asked nervously.

"We go find out who it is," replied Tulio. "And we're going to have to do it fast."

The boys continued further into the drafty tunnel, moving slowly. They rounded a corner and almost bumped into two men who were guarding Samuel the Lamanite and Bear.

They moved back into the tunnel a little way so that they could talk about what to do next.

"We made it in time," whispered Runt.

"Look. They're both still alive," added Tulio.

"What do we do now?" asked Red.

Stick wrinkled his forehead and answered, "I'm not sure."

"They're just tied up. We should be able to untie them," said Red.

"Yes, but how do we get past the guards?" asked Tulio.

"Could we distract them long enough to free Samuel and Bear?" asked Red.

"That's an idea, but we don't have anything to use to cut them free. Plus, how are we going to distract the guards?" asked Stick.

"What about in Tater's backpack? He might have a Swiss army knife or something in his backpack," suggested Stick.

"What about a flashlight? We could flash the light in their eyes and blind them for a minute while we free Samuel and Bear," offered Runt.

"We lost the flashlight, remember?" answered Stick. "It's back in the first tunnel."

"That's right," Runt replied. "That's when I almost died!"

"Stick, Tater always has a bag of smoke bombs and trick stuff. Did you see anything like that when you dried out his backpack?" asked Runt.

Stick sat pondering the question for a moment, then startled the boys when he loudly replied, "Yes, I remember. He did!" Stick quickly started searching the backpack for the small plastic bag.

"Ssssshhhh!" insisted Tulio, as he saw the guards glance toward the boys.

"Sounds like we'll be leaving soon," said one of the guards.

"It's about time. I've had enough of being in these tunnels. I need some sun," replied the other guard, as he leaned his chair back against the wall.

"I think Giddianhi should have to sit down here himself for one day to see what it's like," said the first guard.

"That would be funny, wouldn't it?" asked the other guard. "I bet he couldn't last one day."

The two men laughed at Giddianhi's expense for several minutes, never giving a second thought to the noise in the tunnel.

※

"That was lucky," said Red, as he breathed a sigh of relief. "Be careful, Stick. You're gonna get us caught."

"Look what I found," replied Stick, holding up a small plastic bag.

"What is it?" Runt whispered.

"Well, I can see three smoke bombs and two rows of Silver Crackers," Stick said excitedly. "I am so glad that I ended up here with Tater's backpack, he has everything in here!"

"We are lucky," agreed Runt.

"What are those things you have?" asked Tulio.

"Well, these are flash crackers. When you light them,

they flash bright lights several times. When you light smoke bombs, they fill the area with smoke."

"Oh," replied Tulio in awe.

"Nice," said Runt. "I have an idea."

"What is it?" asked Red.

"Okay, I think we should light the smoke bombs first. When the guards see the smoke, they'll get up to see what is going on. Then we light the flash crackers and throw them toward the guards. They'll be blinded momentarily by the smoke and flashing. Then we can knock them out or something like that," said Runt.

"Good thinking, but I don't have any matches," replied Stick.

"There aren't any in the plastic bag with the fireworks?" Runt asked.

"Nope, not one," replied Stick. "So, unless either of you guys have some, these fireworks aren't going to do us any good," he said holding up the bag.

"I don't have any," Red replied.

"Yeah, neither do I," replied Runt. "I don't usually carry them with me."

"I don't even know what you're talking about," added Tulio. "So, I know that I don't have any."

"Now what?" asked Runt. "I can't think of another plan that might work."

"There has to be something we can do without getting caught," said Tulio. "I could rush in and grab one of them, if you guys could get the other one."

"Then what?" demanded Runt.

"I don't know. It was just a thought," replied Tulio.

"Hey, wait a minute. I think I've got matches in my first aid kit!" Red said excitedly.

"I hadn't thought about looking in a first aid kit. I might have some, too," Runt said, smiling nervously.

"I have a full book," said Red, as he held them up for Stick to see.

"Yes! Good job, Red," said Stick, as he patted Red on the back.

"Okay, I'll light the fireworks. Runt, after smoke fills the room, you and Tulio wait for the lights to flash, then rush in and overtake the two men. Red, once they've done that, run over and release both Bear and Samuel."

"How exactly are we going to overtake them, Stick?" asked Runt.

"I don't know. Do you have anything in your backpack you could hit them with?" asked Stick.

"The only thing that might work is rope. At least we'll be able to tie them up," said Runt, holding up the rope for Tulio to see.

"Maybe you can trip the guards and then tie them up when they're down on the floor," suggested Red.

"That might work," replied Runt. "Good idea, Red," he said, as he handed one end of the rope to Tulio.

"I can hit pretty hard, too. I'll try to knock them out," said Tulio, showing his clenched fist.

Runt grinned widely and nodded his head.

"Okay, is everyone ready?" asked Stick.

He held up the match, ready to strike it against the matchbook.

"Yep, let's do this!" replied Red. "We're running out of time."

Stick nervously whispered. "Good luck, everyone."

He struck the match and the small light instantly threw a shadow across the room. Stick quickly held the flame under the wick. He waited several seconds before the wick on the first smoke bomb finally caught fire.

Soon Stick had all three smoke bombs filling the area with smoke.

Only moments passed before the bright lights from the flash crackers also filled the room. Runt shielded his eyes and carefully counted for all twelve lights to flash before he ran toward the prisoners.

Tulio did not know to shield his eyes and was blinded by the bright flashes. He suddenly felt the rope move and knew that Runt was moving. He tried to follow, but tripped as they entered the small opening.

Fortunately, the guards were stumbling around the room, trying to figure out what was happening. Red and Tulio stretched out the rope, tripping the guards. Both men toppled to the floor, hitting their heads together as they fell. The men were both knocked out by the time they hit the ground.

Chaos ensued. Tulio struggled to regain his vision. His arms flailed wildly in the air. He was trying to find the guard. Runt could see fine, so he quickly tied both hands and feet of the guards who were knocked out and lying on the floor. Red and Stick tried to see through the smoke-filled room. They needed to untie Bear and the prophet, but were unable to see anything.

"Bear, are you alright?" whispered Red.

"Yes and no," he replied.

"I'm so sorry we lost you," continued Red, struggling with the knots in the rope. "One minute you were there, and the next you were gone."

"I know," Bear replied. "I hid inside a small cottage. I was okay the first night, but they caught me the next day."

"What's the matter with the prophet?" asked Stick as he noticed his lifeless body. "Is he okay?"

"No, he's not doing very well," replied Bear. "He's not even strong enough to speak anymore."

"Why?" asked Stick

Stick watched as Bear just shrugged his shoulders and replied, "I think he needs food."

"I can't get these knots untied around his wrists," complained Stick. "I wish I had a knife."

"Neither can I," added Red. "Of course, it doesn't help that I can't see anything."

"I have a little pocket knife in my backpack. Both of the guards also have small hand knives tucked inside their sashes," answered Bear.

"That'll work," said Stick, stumbling toward the men.

"Runt, Bear said they both have knives in their sashes," said Stick. "Can you help me find them?"

Runt searched the men and located the knives. He handed one to Stick and stuck the other one inside his backpack. "Just in case," he thought to himself.

Stick freed Bear and Samuel. In the meantime, Tulio finally got his vision back.

"What happened?" Tulio asked. "I couldn't see a thing."

"I forgot to warn you not to look at the light," replied Stick. "Sorry about that."

"I'm sorry, Runt. I tried to help," Tulio said apologetically.

Runt could see the devastated look on Tulio's face. "Are you kidding, Tulio? You helped tons!" he replied.

"I did?" he asked excitedly.

"You sure did," Runt answered. "I couldn't have tied the guards up if you hadn't helped trip them and knocked them to the floor with all your hitting and kicking."

"That's all I could think to do," replied Tulio.

"Well, you did great!" said Runt.

Chapter Eighteen

"Runt, Tulio, I need your help!" yelled Stick. "I can't even get the prophet to stand."

The two boys hurried to help Stick. Tulio grabbed the prophet's arm and hoisted him to his feet.

"We've got to hurry. The smoke is starting to clear," said Runt.

"We've got to get out of here before the guards wake up," said Tulio, trembling with fear.

"Where? How?" asked Red. "We're never going to be able to sneak out if we've got to carry Samuel like this."

"There is another tunnel—one that is not very far from here," answered Bear. "I overheard one of the guards talking about how fun it is to float in the water all the way down into the River Sidon."

"Are you serious?" asked Stick. "Float?"

"Yes, only I'm not sure which tunnel," replied Bear.

"I don't think I care. I'm not getting into any more water in this city. My feet are still killing me," replied Stick.

"My feet, too," agreed Red. "Every step hurts."

Bear, confused at why their feet hurt, asked, "Why? What happened?"

"That's a story for another time," replied Runt. "We don't have time for that right now."

"You two are going to have to get over your fear. If this is the only tunnel we can use to get out of here without being caught, we're going to take it, piranha or not," insisted Runt.

"Piranha?" asked Bear. "Are there piranhas in the water here?"

"Yep! Stick and I already had a run in with them," replied Red.

"What is the matter with the prophet, Bear?" interrupted Tulio.

"Dehydration, I think," he replied. "I don't think he has had any food and barely any water for at least three or four days."

"We're never going to make it out of here, back through this tunnel," said Stick. "We've got to find another way."

"Think carefully. What exactly did the guard say?" asked Tulio. "We've got to get the prophet out of here as quickly as we can. He can hardly walk."

"All I can remember is that the tunnel is a little cooler than the others," said Bear.

"There was a tunnel that had a draft, remember?"

asked Tulio. "We didn't know what it was."

"It wasn't too far from here," said Runt. "Let's hurry."

"Tulio, help me with Samuel. Runt, Red and Bear, you lead the way," insisted Stick.

"Should I get the glow stick out of my backpack?" asked Red. "We might be able to see a little better."

"And maybe we can find where we need to go a little faster," added Bear.

"Yeah, that might really help us," replied Stick, as he pulled the prophet's arm around his shoulder.

Red quickly found the glow stick and the boys started cautiously down the tunnel. As they reached the first side passage, Red quickly stepped inside, hoping to feel cool air.

"No change in here," he quietly called.

"Let's keep going. I remember a really cool breeze," said Tulio.

"Are you guys doing all right?" asked Runt, noticing Stick and Tulio struggling with the weight of the prophet.

"We're doing okay. Keep going. We've got to find the tunnel out of here," replied Stick.

Runt continued to push forward, trying to locate the next passageway. As he did, he stepped inside, but, again he felt no change in the temperature.

"It's not this tunnel either, Tulio," called Runt.

"Are you sure?" he called. "I don't remember it being very far."

"I can't feel any temperature change," Runt replied.

"Then keep going. We'll catch up with you," called Stick. "Just find it quick, before those guards sound the alarm."

"Or the men from the meeting come in here to get the prophet and catch us," Runt mumbled under his breath.

The three boys hurried to the next passage and then to the next, unable to find a passage with a breeze or any sort of change in temperature.

"Be careful, it's the gooey, mud tunnel again," said Red, as he felt it ooze through his toes.

Once they were through the mud, they hurried further into the tunnel checking for any sign of cool air.

"Something's not right," said Red. "I'm sure the tunnel with the breeze wasn't this far."

"Run back and tell others to wait where they are until we find the tunnel," suggested Runt. "There's no reason to drag the prophet all over until we figure out where we need to go."

"By myself?" gasped Red.

"Come on, Red! There's only a hundred feet or so between us. Just move it," demanded Runt.

Red ran as fast as his legs could carry him, back toward Stick. Just as he saw their shadows, he unexpectedly ran into the thick, gooey mud on the floor. Without any warning, his feet were suddenly stuck, and he slammed face-first into the ground. Stick and Tulio watched everything that happened and chuckled as he fell. Stick saw how hard he fell and knew how bad it had to hurt, so he tried not to laugh too much.

"Red, buddy, are you alright?"

With no immediate response, Stick again called, "Red, are you hurt?"

"What do you think, Stick?" Red snapped, as he forcefully pulled his head from the mud.

With a sudden pop as his head snapped free, Stick could no longer control his laughter.

"That was a great crash, buddy. It was almost as good as when you hit the rock that was hidden underneath the puddle back at Mr. Jensen's house."

"Real funny, Stick," Red retorted, as he wiped the mud from his eyes, nose and mouth. "You know, that kinda hurt a little."

"I'm sure it did," Stick replied, still snickering. "The only thing that could have made the fall better is if you would have flipped over once before you landed face-first in the mud."

"Ha, ha, ha, Stick," Red sarcastically replied, kneeling on the ground and wiping more mud from his face. "You know, there is mud up my nose."

"Oh, I'm sorry, Red," laughed Stick. "I know it's not funny, but it sure looked funny."

"Yeah, I know. This would have been a great shot for America's Funniest Home Videos, right?"

"I think you would have won!" Stick answered.

"Can I help you up?" asked Tulio, as they finally reached Red, who was still on the ground.

"No, thanks," he replied, as he put his hands down in the wet mud and slowly started to push himself up off the ground.

"Hey, I can feel the cool air. This is the tunnel we need," Red said excitedly. "I forgot we were crawling when we felt the air before."

"Nice job, Red," said Stick. "I guess you needed to fall to find the right tunnel."

"You know, Stick when we get home, you're so gonna get it," warned Red.

"I know," he replied, smiling.

"You two take the prophet and follow this tunnel. I'll get Runt and Bear, and we'll catch up with you," insisted Red.

"Are you sure?" asked Tulio. "I'm not excited about being separated."

"I'm sure. Now hurry, and get moving," Red replied, as he ran to find the others.

"Runt, Bear, where are you?" Red called softly. "Guys, come on. Where are you?"

Red followed the tunnel fifty yards before he finally caught up with Bear and Runt.

"Come on. I found the right tunnel. Hurry!" insisted Red.

"Wait a minute. Listen," said Runt, holding onto Red's arm.

"What? What is it?" asked Red. "I don't want to wait."

"I can hear Captain Gilead's speech. He's trying to talk mean, it's almost funny," Runt replied. "I think it's echoing in here."

"I don't care what he's saying," snapped Red. "Let's get out of here!"

"He's right, Runt. Let's go," insisted Bear. "I don't like any of those guys."

"You're right," replied Runt. "Let's get out of here."

"Hey, wait. What happened to you?" asked Bear.

"Oh, nothing," Red replied.

"Why are you all muddy?" persisted Runt.

"I was playing in the mud and I thought it would be

fun to wipe all over myself," Red replied sarcastically.

"Did you fall or something?" pressed Bear.

"Just come on. Follow me," Red replied, ignoring the question.

"Did you find the right tunnel?" asked Runt.

"I think so," Red answered. "We felt the cool air when we were crawling before, remember?"

"Wow, nice job. I can't believe you remembered that," said Runt. "Red, lead the way."

Red began running as fast as he could. When he was sure he was getting close to the right tunnel, he slowed down. He did not want to have another fall like the last one.

"What are you doing? Why are you slowing down?" asked Bear.

"The tunnel we're looking for is by the spot where the dirt turns muddy," replied Red. "I already fell once. I don't want to do it again."

Bear smiled and asked, "So, I was right? You did fall!"

"Yes, and it didn't feel too great," snapped Red. "So, quit teasing me."

The boys moved slowly for about ten feet when Bear said, "I found it—it's right here. Now where do we go?"

"This is the tunnel with the cool air, like you said, Bear. I already told Tulio and Stick to start down this passage, and that we would catch up with them as soon as we could," replied Red.

"Look behind us," said Bear nervously. "Lights?"

"No, those are torches. The evil men are on their way up here to get you. Come on. We've got to go," insisted Runt. "It's only going to be seconds before they're know you're gone and they start searching for you and Samuel."

"We've got to hurry. I don't want to get caught again," replied Bear.

Bear grabbed Runt's shirt and started pulling. They hurried through the tunnel for several minutes before they finally caught up with Tulio and Stick.

"We've got to move faster," Runt whispered into Stick's ear. "They were on their way to get the prisoners, just as we started running down this passage."

"Do you want to move ahead of us and see if you can find where we need to go?" asked Tulio.

"I can, but I'd rather stay behind you and make sure I'm here to help," Runt replied.

"Okay. Why don't you do that, and we'll have Red and Bear scout ahead of us," suggested Stick. "We may need some help back here, the prophet seems to be getting weaker and weaker by the minute."

"I'll tell them," said Runt, as he hurried to catch the two boys.

Red and Bear agreed and hurried deeper into the tunnel. They searched desperately for water so that they could float to freedom. While Stick and Tulio continued to help Samuel, Runt kept watch behind them.

Suddenly, several loud yells echoed through the tunnels. The boys knew instantly that Captain Gilead's men had discovered the prisoners had escaped and were on the move.

"Captain! Captain!" yelled Shiz. "They've escaped."

"What do you mean they've escaped?" he yelled angrily.

"We went to get them, and they were gone," Shiz replied.

"Aaauuuggghhh! How did this happen?" he screamed at the top of his lungs.

"The two soldiers on guard don't know how it happened. They said they were standing guard when smoke started to fill the room. They began to investigate when, suddenly, there was a bright flash of light. The next thing they knew we were waking them up and the prisoners were gone," Shiz explained.

"Who helped them?" demanded Captain Gilead.

"Could it have been Nephi?" asked Lib.

"How could it have been?" asked Ethem. "No one knows how to navigate these tunnels besides the Gadianton robbers."

"This makes no sense!" yelled Captain Gilead. "Just find them. Whoever has helped them will join in the prophet's fate."

Lighting several torches, the men began searching the tunnel for any sign that might lead them to the escaped prisoners and their accomplices.

"Morihan, take five men and search this passage," ordered Giddianhi. "Shiz, do the same. Take five men and search this tunnel," he said, pointing to another passageway.

"But, Sir, you know that tunnel is a trap," replied Shiz. "If they tried to escape in there, they're either dead already, or they will have to come back out here."

"I don't care. We're going to search every tunnel for

them!" he demanded. "They will not make a fool of me in front of Captain Gilead."

"Yes, Sir," replied Shiz. He motioned for five men to follow him, and they began searching inside the passage.

"Lib, you take five men and start searching in this tunnel. Ethem, you take five and start looking in the next," ordered Commander Giddianhi.

"Yes, Sir," both men replied, motioning for the soldiers to follow them.

"I can't believe this," Giddianhi muttered under his breath. "Who helped them escape?"

As Giddianhi made his way over to the men who had been guarding the prisoners, he stepped through the mud. One of his men noticed the passageway.

"Sir, what about this tunnel?" he asked.

"I will search that tunnel myself after I question the guards," he answered abruptly. "Now, where are they?"

"Right here, Sir," said another soldier, pointing to the men tied up on the floor.

Commander Giddianhi squatted down so that he could look into the guards faces. Then he asked, "Would someone please tell me how an old, sick man and a child escaped from two very big, strong soldiers?"

"I don't know," muttered one of the guards. "One minute everything was fine, and the next, we were surrounded by smoke, then blinded and knocked unconscious."

"What do you mean, blinded?" demanded Giddianhi.

"It was dark in here, as usual. Then suddenly, the room was filled with bright flashes of light," the guard replied.

"Was the light from torches?" asked Giddianhi.

"No, Sir. The light seemed brighter than the sun," he replied. "It was as if the Lord was angry and threw light from the heavens, so that the man and boy could go free."

"Then how did you come to be tied up," yelled Giddianhi angrily. "Did you see or hear anything?"

"No, Sir, not a word," replied the guard. "Well, we did hear a small sound just before smoke filled the room. We thought some of the men were on their way to take the prisoners to the ceremony."

"I knew it! Someone helped them escape. You did not see a light from the heavens. You were tricked by someone," reasoned Giddianhi.

"I'm sorry, Sir. I didn't see anyone come to help them escape," the guard said timidly.

"Silence! You two fools are lucky I don't kill you right here," Giddianhi snapped. "Have any of the men found anything yet?" he yelled back into the tunnel.

"Nothing yet, Sir," replied a voice in the distance.

"Cut these two men free," ordered Giddianhi. "You two and three more men follow me. We've got a rat here in the tunnels, and I intend to find and kill him."

Giddianhi turned abruptly and headed back down the passageway, stomping quickly through the thick, sticky mud toward the tunnel.

"Men, look everywhere. The prisoners will not escape from here today, or you will not remain alive," he warned, angrily swinging his sword against the tunnel wall, sending a spark of light flashing as the sword struck a rock.

Chapter Nineteen

"I can hear them. They're not far behind," warned Runt, as he looked over his shoulder.

"I think you're hearing echoes," Stick replied nervously.

"Bear, Red, any luck finding water yet?" asked Tulio.

"Not yet," Red answered. "But we can hear water coming from somewhere. We've got to be close."

"Hurry! We can hear them in the tunnel behind us," said Tulio. "Keep searching."

"We're trying," Bear replied.

The words had barely left Bear's mouth when the boys rounded another corner in the tunnel and entered a large open area. The area was filled with lush, green plants and sweet-smelling flowers. Out of the north wall poured a beautiful waterfall. The water flowed almost transparently down the rock wall and into a crystal-clear lake below. It flowed quickly out of the small lake into a fast moving stream, and finally disappeared underneath the west side of the tunnel.

"Stick, Runt, Tulio, I think we found it!" Bear called excitedly.

The boys carried the prophet even faster, excited by the news.

"Bear, you were right. You've saved us!" called Runt, as he rushed to the water's edge.

"Check for piranha, Runt," called Tulio. "Don't get in until you look!"

Runt stopped and quickly jumped back from the water's edge.

"Thanks, Tulio," he called. "I forgot."

"Can you believe that waterfall?" asked Red. "I've never seen anything like it."

"The water looks almost like diamonds, the way it sparkles off the wall, and lands in the lake below," said Bear, in awe of the area's beauty.

"Who would have thought anything like this existed anywhere," said Runt.

"You should, after seeing the caves we found when we were searching for Moroni's treasure," replied Stick. "Don't you remember the area we found that was a lot like this?" "Yes, I do," replied Red. "I just don't remember the water being so pretty."

"Well, I don't remember any of it," said Bear, as he looked at the water.

"You weren't with us when we found it, Bear. Maybe someday we'll get to show you," replied Red. "It was almost as beautiful as this."

"Do you think that area we found and this area are the same place, just thousands of years apart?" asked Runt.

"Possibly, but we don't have time to figure that out right now," said Stick, as he and Tulio finally joined the others at the water's edge.

"I think we should leave a mark or something we can use to check when we get back home," said Runt.

"With what? And how are we going to mark something?" asked Red.

"I don't know? Do you have any ideas?" Runt asked.

"I have an idea," replied Bear.

"Okay, what's you're idea?" asked Red.

"What if we dug a hole over by that rock with all the hieroglyphics and buried a baseball?" replied Bear.

"Would the baseball last for thousands of years?" asked Runt.

"Probably not," replied Stick. "And we don't have time to mess with that, anyway."

"But, Stick," said Bear. "Think how cool it would be to find the baseball back home."

Stick looked at Bear, then over his shoulder at the tunnel behind them, and replied. "Can you see any piranha, Runt? We've got to go."

"No, nothing yet. I think we're okay," he replied nervously.

"Good. What do we do now?" Stick asked, looking at Bear.

"I'm not sure. The guard said you get in the water and float," Bear answered quietly.

"Bear, if you want to get caught, by all means go over to the rock and bury the baseball," started Stick. "Just know, we are not going to save you again."

"Thanks, Stick," called Bear as he ran down nearly twenty feet to the water's edge. There, just out of the water was a mammoth rock covered in hieroglyphics. He frantically started digging the sand away from the base of the rock. As the other boys watched Bear struggle with the sand, Stick said, "Runt, Red, why don't you two help him before we're all caught."

Excitedly, Runt and Red raced to help Bear with the sand. They had the hole more than eighteen inches deep in no time at all.

"Do you think that's deep enough, Runt?" asked Bear.

"Who cares?" answered Red. "Just hurry up and put the ball in there, Bear."

"Yeah, we don't have time to waste, Bear," agreed Runt.

Bear dropped the ball inside the hole and they quickly pushed the sand over it, completely filling the opening.

Stick shook his head as he watched the three boys rush back towards him.

"Okay, Bear tell me again, did the guards say what they did when they got to the water?" asked Stick.

"No, just that they floated in the water," Bear replied.

"Do you think they meant just floating around in this lake?" asked Red.

"I don't think so," Bear replied.

"Float to where? This looks like a small lake," snapped Stick, nervous that Giddianhi's men were very close behind.

"I don't know. They said the water would take them all the way out to the River Sidon," replied Bear.

"We've got to try something," insisted Tulio. "I can hear the soldiers' footsteps. They're not far away."

"The water in the lake has to drain somewhere. This entire area would be completely filled with all the water that is pouring in here from the waterfall if it didn't," Red reasoned.

"I think we should get in the water and see what happens," suggested Runt.

"And what if we get pulled under by a strong current and we all drown?" Stick asked angrily. "Then what?"

"I guess that will be better than being caught by either Giddianhi or Captain Gilead," replied Tulio. He quickly lowered himself into the water, pulling the prophet in as well. He wrapped his arms around Samuel, trying to hold his head above the water.

"I agree," added Bear. "I hope I never see those men again."

"We've got to try something, Stick," urged Red.

"Even if it means we're just floating in the water when the soldiers get in here?" asked Stick.

"Yes," replied Runt. "Now, come on. We're out of options."

Runt pulled at Stick's shirt until he finally agreed.

The boys floated uneventfully for several moments. The current in the water was mild and barely moved them around.

"I told you nothing would happen," said Stick, frustrated that nothing was happening.

"Patience," said Tulio. "Be patient. Let the water move you around, don't try to move yourself in the water."

"Is Samuel okay?" Bear asked nervously, as he looked at the prophet. "He doesn't look like he's doing very well."

"He's still breathing," replied Tulio. "But I think he needs food and water as soon as possible."

"Do you need any help?" asked Runt, trying to maneuver his way toward them.

"No! Hold still," Tulio insisted. "I can feel something."

"Me, too," said Bear.

"What is it?" asked Stick. "Are there piranha in here?"

Suddenly, Bear's head slipped under the water and then popped right back up.

"Are you okay, Bear?" Stick asked worriedly. "Do you need some help? Are you tired?"

"I'm fin…," he started, as his head again disappeared underneath the water, this time without resurfacing.

"What's going on here?" asked Red. "Where did he go? Some one, quick! Save him!"

"Do I need to go under and find him?" asked Stick.

"I'm not sure," replied Red.

"Hey, where did Tulio and the prophet go?" asked Stick, glancing back to where they had just been floating. "I only took my eyes off them for a second."

"What's happening here?" Runt asked anxiously.

"Could the current be taking them out of here?" asked Stick.

"Quiet, Stick," insisted Red. "Look! Here come the soldiers," he said, pointing toward the tunnel.

"And there is Giddian...," started Runt, suddenly disappearing underneath the water, too.

"I think if we hold really still, the underwater current will take us," whispered Red.

"I sure hope so," replied Stick.

He looked at Giddianhi's large sword and noticed the anger clearly displayed on his face. Stick watched as Red suddenly disappeared underneath the water and wondered why the current had not taken him yet.

"Search, men!" yelled Giddianhi, as they entered the open area. "Spread out! Check behind every plant and rock. They've got to be hiding in here somewhere!"

"Sir?" said one of the guards.

"I said search!" Giddianhi snapped.

"Yes, Sir," the guard replied nervously, as he turned and started looking around.

Stick quietly watched as Giddianhi wandered through the trees and plants trying to locate the escapees, swinging his sword like a machete as he searched.

Several minutes passed in silence before he yelled, "Where are they?"

"There is no sign of them in this tunnel, Sir," replied one of the soldiers. "Should we turn back and see if any of the other men have located them yet?"

"NO!" he screamed. "They are in here, I can feel it. Keep searching! Leave no stone unturned!"

"Sir?" the guard timidly said again.

"What? What is it?" Giddianhi demanded.

"The boy prisoner could have overheard me talking," he replied.

"And what does that mean?" asked Giddianhi, pointing the edge of his sword at the guard's neck.

"Well, Sir," he started quietly.

"Speak up," interrupted Giddianhi. "What are you trying to say?"

"I have been in this tunnel before. I was telling the other guard about the time when I was swimming in the water and an underwater current pulled me under. Amazingly, I ended up in the River Sidon," he explained.

"Oh, no! I'm dead now," thought Stick as he closed his eyes tightly and prayed that the men could not see him.

"This water?" asked Giddianhi, pointing with his sword.

"Yes, Sir," the guard replied.

Finally, Stick felt the current start to pull his legs, and he suddenly disappeared underneath the water.

"Then you get in there and see if they have used this route to escape," replied Giddianhi.

"I don't think anyone else knew about the current but me," the guard replied.

"Did I say I cared if anyone else but you knew?"

Giddianhi screamed. "No, I didn't. I told you to get in there and see if you could find the prisoners."

"Yes, Sir." the guard replied. He walked quickly to the water's edge and got in and began to float.

Giddianhi watched skeptically as the man floated around for nearly five minutes, then, suddenly, disappeared under the water.

"Is he dead?" asked Giddianhi nervously. "No one can survive underneath the water for that long."

"I think he said that the current pulled him out to the River Sidon," replied a soldier.

Giddianhi glared at the soldier without saying a word. Then he swung his sword in the air and yelled, "Men, have you found any sign of them?"

"No," echoed through the tunnel.

"Then let's return to see if they've been found by any of the other men," he replied.

"Sir, what about the water?" asked a soldier. "Could they have escaped that way?"

"I don't know, but I'm going to find out," he replied. "Return to Ethem, and advise him to meet me at the River Sidon. If it is true that the pond empties into the river, I will make it there alive. Then we will capture the prisoners, and kill the rat that helped them to escape, too."

"I will tell him, Sir," replied the soldier.

He watched Giddianhi enter the cool water. Giddianhi floated patiently for several minutes, before he, too, finally disappeared under the water. Once he was gone, his men ran to tell Ethem what Commander Giddianhi had said.

Ethem, upon hearing the news, assembled several men, including Shiz, Lib and Morihan. He informed Captain Gilead of his plans, and then headed out of the tunnels.

"I can't believe this, Ethem," said Shiz. "No outsider has ever found a way into the tunnels, let alone back out again."

"I know. Something doesn't seem right, does it?" replied Ethem.

"Do you think we have a spy pretending to be one of us?" asked Lib.

"I don't know," answered Ethem. "But I do know that Captain Gilead's anger is worse than I have ever seen."

"Do you think Nephi could have found his way down into the tunnels?" asked Morihan.

"I didn't think anyone could, but I guess it's possible," Ethem replied suspiciously.

"I thought we had Nephi under constant surveillance," said Shiz.

"We did until a few hours before the scheduled ceremony," replied Morihan. "Then we stopped watching him to attend."

"I'm not sure that was such a good idea, now," replied Lib.

"Do you think I need to go to Nephi's secret house now?" asked Morihan. "We could wait to see if the prophet or boy show up?"

"No, let's wait and if Giddianhi makes it to the river alive, we'll get our orders from him," replied Ethem.

The men maneuvered their way out of the tunnels

and into the city. Ethem shielded his eyes for several moments, as they adjusted to the afternoon light. He quickly scanned the area, hoping to somehow find the escaped prisoners and return them to the ceremony. With no sign of the prisoners anywhere, Ethem clenched his fist in frustration and hit the High Priests Temple wall with his hand. He turned and with the men started toward the River Sidon.

"Did Giddianhi say how long he thought getting through the water would take?" asked Ethem.

"No, I don't think he even had a clue if he would live through being pulled under the water," replied Shiz.

"Isn't that Nephi?" asked Morihan, pointing toward the market.

"Yes, I believe it is," replied Lib.

"Should we take him for questioning?" asked Shiz.

"What are we going to question him about?" asked Ethem.

"If he didn't do it, then who helped those prisoners escape?" questioned Morihan.

"Probably one of his followers," replied Morihan.

The men hurried toward the river. They were completely unaware that Nephi had spotted them and was now following. The men reached the river and quickly started searching the shoreline for any sign of the escaped prisoners, the guard, or their Commander, Giddianhi. Searching the area a mile south of town and a mile north of town, the men found absolutely no sign of anyone.

❋

Sputtering and coughing, Stick finally surfaced. He looked around anxiously and soon spotted Tulio, the prophet, Red, Runt, and Bear about thirty yards away from where he was.

"Are we alive?" he called, smiling.

"What took you so long?" asked Red.

"I don't know," Stick replied. "Is everyone alright?"

"We're fine," replied Runt.

"And Samuel?" asked Stick, looking at Tulio.

"Weak, but alive," Tulio replied.

"Where are we?" asked Stick, as he looked around.

"I have no idea," replied Red. "All I know is that we are no longer being chased by Giddianhi's men."

"Actually, I think we are," said Stick. "Just before the current took me under the water, the guard that Bear overheard talking, told Giddianhi about the current."

"Are you serious?" asked Bear. "I was hoping that he wouldn't find out."

"No such luck. Giddianhi knows," replied Stick. "I'm sure of it."

"Now what?" asked Runt.

"We get moving as fast as we can," replied Tulio, still holding the weak prophet. "I don't want to get caught now, especially after everything we've been through."

The boys floated through the dark tunnel, unable to see where they were or where they were going.

"Red do you still have that glow stick?" asked Runt. "I'm tired of not being able to see anything."

"Yeah," he replied. "I think so."

"I'd love to be able to see where we going," Runt said sarcastically.

"Then people will be able to see us," Red replied nervously.

"That's all right," Runt replied, splashing water toward the sound of Red's voice.

"We'll also be able to see them coming," replied Red.

Red reached into the side pocket of his backpack and pulled out the still faintly-glowing light stick.

As the boy's eyes adjusted to the light, they realized they were floating through a tunnel ten feet wide and eight feet tall.

"I didn't know we were moving this fast, until I could see the walls of the tunnel flying by," said Stick, a little frightened.

"You know, with as fast as were moving, if there were big rocks under the surface, we might have white water rapids. I bet we'd be at least in class three rapids," added Bear.

"Everybody hanging in there okay?" asked Stick.

"I'm getting really tired," replied Tulio.

"Do you need me to take a turn holding onto Samuel?" asked Stick, trying to maneuver toward Tulio.

"No, not yet," Tulio replied. "But maybe soon."

"Hey, everyone, look!" Red yelled, as he pointed to the tunnel wall.

"What is it?" Runt asked nervously. "What do you see?"

"More hieroglyphics—a lot of them," Red yelled.

"Cool, but Red, don't scream like that unless someone's about to catch us, okay?" Bear insisted angrily. "I just about had a heart attack."

"Sorry, but look at them. I can see hundreds of them," Red replied.

"I wonder what they mean?" said Bear.

"You know, if we had a camera, we could snap some pictures and take them back to Cheri, so she could translate them," suggested Red.

"That would be cool!" replied Runt. "I wish I had a camera."

"Yeah, me, too," added Stick. "I'd like to have a picture of the city and the river."

"I wonder if the hieroglyphics give information about the people mentioned in the *Book of Mormon*?" said Bear.

"Could be," replied Runt.

"Look at the lower walls of the tunnel," said Tulio, as he pointed.

"They are lined with handmade pots and vases," said Runt. "I wonder why?"

"Do you think people hid down here?" asked Red.

"I don't know," answered Runt.

"I read once that pots and vases were left in tunnels as a sacrifice," said Stick.

"By whom?" asked Bear.

"I don't know," Stick replied, shrugging his shoulders.

"Look at the walls. Behind the writing, they sparkle with something. And what is that stuff on the ceiling?" quizzed Tulio.

"Look!" said Stick, pointing at the ceiling. "Stalagmites

or stalactites. I can't remember what they're called, but they sure are cool."

"They're not as long as those ones we saw back home," said Runt.

"They're not as old, Runt," replied Red. "Of course they're not as long!"

"I'm cold, Stick," said Bear. "When can we get out of here?"

"Stick, why are the walls closing in on us?" asked Runt.

"I don't know," replied Stick. "It looks like we're headed underneath the water again."

"Hey, we're picking up speed," said Tulio. "Stick, you better get over here and help me keep the prophet's head above water as much as possible."

Stick moved as fast as he could toward Tulio and grabbed a hold of the prophet's arm. Suddenly, a scream sounded behind the boys.

"Oh, no! It sounds like we've got company," said Red.

He glanced over his shoulder, trying to see who had screamed. As he did, the tunnel floor unexpectedly gave way and the boys were rapidly floating down hill.

"Now, these are some class five rapids!" yelled Bear. He slammed into the side of the tunnel, grunting as the water forced him further through the area.

"Huuuuhh," squealed Red, as the water threw him against the wall.

"Uuuggghhh," called Stick, as he cushioned the wall for the prophet.

"I can't do this anymore!" screamed Red.

"You have to," replied Stick.

"Hold on. We've got to be close," replied Runt.

"Stick, I can't hold on," yelled Tulio.

"I've got him," Stick replied. He quickly moved his arms around the prophet's chest and locked his fingers closed.

The boys continued moving at a rapid pace for the next few minutes and then the tunnel funneled them under the water. They were pushed through a small hole and ended up in a large, open area filled with white, sandy beaches, palm trees and birds.

"Should we climb out here and hide?' asked Red.

"Even if we could get over to the side in this fast moving water, how would we escape?" asked Runt.

"I don't know, but someone is behind us," replied Red. "What do we do about that?"

"If we get out onto the riverbank and we find no way to escape, then we are caught for sure," responded Tulio.

"He's right. At least in the water we're moving and whoever is following us shouldn't be able to catch us," said Stick.

"But, there is light in here. There has to be someway to escape and hide," said Bear. "I'm still freezing."

"The light doesn't look like sunlight, though," insisted Stick. "It looks like man-made light."

"I bet someone lives up there or has lived here before," replied Tulio. "People do it all the time so that they don't have to answer to the Chief Judge or Ruler."

"We've floated nearly thirty minutes or more in this water. Do you think we're getting close to the river?" asked Bear, shivering from the cool water.

"We've got to be," Runt replied anxiously. "Can't you feel the current picking up again?"

"Not again," squealed Red. "I'm not that good of a swimmer."

"Well, I am, Red. And even I'm starting to get tired," said Bear, trying to reassure him.

Stick felt the current start to get stronger and stronger as the walls of the tunnel moved by faster and faster.

"I can see them, Stick," said Tulio.

"See who?" he asked.

"Two soldiers following us," Tulio replied.

"They're catching up with us!" yelled Bear. "They're going to catch us."

"No, they're not," replied Stick, matter-of-factly.

"How do you know?" asked Red.

"Cause here we go again!" he screamed, as the current pulled the boys down a rock slide, which dropped about fifteen feet.

"This reminds me of an amusement park ride," squealed Bear, as he dipped under the water for a second. "A ride where you get really wet!" he yelled, as he resurfaced.

"There it is!" called Tulio.

"There what is?" asked Stick.

"The light from the sun," he replied.

"Okay, once we're outside, we've got to have a plan," insisted Stick. "Chances are that Giddianhi and his men will be waiting for us."

"What do we do?" asked Red.

"I don't know for sure. I've been thinking, and

there's no way that Giddianhi will know exactly where we'll come out, right?" asked Stick.

"You better hurry. We're almost there!" yelled Tulio.

"We've got to get to the shore as quickly as we can and run up to the jungle. The jungle is the only protection around," said Stick.

"Hold up Samuel's head!" yelled Runt. "We're going under again."

The tunnel rapidly reduced in size, and the boys shot out over a waterfall and into the River Sidon, ten feet below.

"I'm not sure I really like this ride," said Runt, as he surfaced and quickly scanned the area.

"We're further south than when we first got here," said Bear. "Look, the suspension bridge is back that way."

"Everyone, hurry and get to the shore. We need to hide in the cover of the trees before we are seen," insisted Stick. "Tulio, help me carry Samuel, I can't do it alone."

Once everyone was out of the water, they raced toward the safety of the jungle.

Chapter Twenty

"Look, Runt," whispered Stick. "There are some soldiers just beyond the bridge."

"This is so not cool," replied Runt. "How are we ever going to get out of here?"

Stick shrugged his shoulders and scrunched down behind some trees.

"Now what?" asked Bear quietly.

"I don't know," Stick replied nervously.

"You know, any minute now, two more soldiers are going to pop up out of that water and know exactly where we are," Runt reminded the group.

"We've got to get Samuel to Nephi, or to someone who can help him," added Tulio. "He's not doing very well."

"Where? Who?" asked Red. "All that I can see out here

are trees, vines and plants—not anyone who is going to help us."

"Maybe this is where we ask for help," suggested Runt. "We've done everything we can do to save the prophet. Now it's okay to ask the Lord for guidance and help, right?"

"Good idea, Runt," replied Red.

"Stick, since you're the oldest, will you say a prayer?" asked Bear.

"I'd love to," he replied.

Stick asked everyone to kneel down, then quickly said a prayer, asking the Lord for help. When he was finished, the boys looked around, hoping to see something miraculous, but nothing had changed.

"There they are," Tulio whispered frantically.

"Who, the soldiers?" asked Red.

"Yes, the soldiers that were behind us in the water," replied Tulio. "They just surfaced. Can you see them?"

"Yes," Red replied.

"Now what?" asked Runt.

"I have no idea," replied Stick.

"Hey, guys," called Bear, who was sitting on the ground with his backpack in his lap.

"Yeah, Bear?" replied Runt.

"What does it mean when the symbols and words change on the Liahona?" he quietly asked.

"Huh, I totally forgot about the Liahona," said Stick. "It will show us what the Lord wants us to do."

"That and our scriptures," replied Runt, holding his up for everyone to see.

"What is on the Liahona?" asked Stick, crawling quickly toward Bear.

"There is a scripture reference," replied Bear.

"What is it?" asked Runt.

"Helaman chapter sixteen, verse two," he replied.

"I've got it. Let me read it," Runt replied.

"No, wait. We can't right now, the men are climbing out of the water. We've got to go," insisted Tulio. "One of the men is Giddianhi."

"The other is one of the guards who held me prisoner," added Bear.

The boys watched nervously as Giddianhi called for his soldiers to join him.

"Did you catch them, Commander?" asked Ethem.

"Can you see them?" Giddianhi snapped.

"Sorry, Sir," said Ethem. "Did you see how many there were?"

"Several—more than I thought would help that old fool," Giddianhi rudely replied, squeezing the water from his clothes.

"Should we start searching for them?" asked Shiz.

"Yes, search!" he yelled. "And the soldier who brings them back to me will receive a reward of gold."

The soldiers yelled out in excitement and quickly started searching.

"Man alive," said Runt. "When is this guy ever gonna give up?"

"Why does he want to kill Samuel so badly?" asked Bear.

"I can answer that," replied a deep voice from behind the boys.

Startled, they turned around to see who was talking. Stick's heart raced, sure they had been caught.

"Nephi?" asked Tulio.

"Yes, son," he replied.

"I'm so glad to see you," Tulio replied.

"You boys are in serious trouble here," said Nephi, as he peered beyond the trees to see Giddianhi's men searching.

"How did you know we were here?" asked Tulio.

"The Lord works in mysterious ways," he replied smiling. "Especially when you are trying to save His prophets!"

Nephi moved to where Samuel was lying on the ground. He felt for a pulse and looked in his eyes, then lifted Samuel up and threw him over his shoulder.

"Is he going to be alright?" Bear asked nervously.

"Yes, he will be fine," replied Nephi. "Now hurry and follow me. We've got to get back inside the city."

"How are we going to do that?" asked Runt.

Nephi turned and smiled at the boys. "You'll see," he said. "There were a few pluses to being the Chief Judge. I can tell you where secret tunnels are, that not even the Gadianton robbers know about."

"Another tunnel?" asked Bear. "I can't get in the water again. It's too cold."

"There is no water in this tunnel," Nephi replied.

Nephi headed toward Zarahemla's mighty wall. Following closely behind, the boys watched as Nephi pushed through some trees and vines that had grown over the large wall. Afraid they were going to be caught at any moment, the boys stayed as close as they could to Nephi.

Nephi carefully held back some large vines and said, "Hurry! Climb in and stand next to the wall."

Nephi was the last to climb through the vines. They were now completely hidden from the soldiers who were searching through the jungle.

"By the way, boys," Nephi began, as he lowered Samuel to the ground, "don't ever ditch me again."

"Sorry about that, Nephi," replied Red. "That was my fault. I saw Giddianhi dragging Bear across the open market, and I couldn't just stand there and do nothing."

Nephi smiled and turned to face Red. Placing his hand on Red's shoulder, Nephi replied, "I know. You are a good friend. Just don't do that to me again!"

Red nodded. Nephi turned back toward the wall. "There is a secret passage here somewhere," he mumbled, searching around for something.

"Can we help you look?" asked Stick, afraid the soldiers would find them at any moment.

"Sure," replied Nephi. "I am looking for a stone engraved with a small scarab."

"A scarab? Those things are so disgusting," said Runt.

"Ssshhh," whispered Nephi. "We're not safe yet. We must be quiet."

"I found it," Stick called softly. "I found the stone."

"Good job, son," replied Nephi. "Now watch this."

Nephi looked at the boys and smiled, then gently pushed the small bug into the wall. Suddenly, a small doorway opened at the base of the wall.

"Follow me quickly, boys," insisted Nephi, as he carefully carried the prophet inside the opening.

Stick climbed in last. As soon as he was through the doorway, Nephi said. "Now, push the scarab back out and close the opening."

Stick quickly pushed the scarab stone and watched as the concrete opening slid closed.

"I can't see anything," said Bear, as he searched for someone to hold on to.

"I still have the glow stick," said Red. He pulled it from his pants pocket and held it up for everyone to see. "It's starting to lose some of its power, but I think it will help us see a little."

"Yes, that will work," said Nephi, as he started down the tunnel.

"Nephi, what is this tunnel?" asked Stick.

"This tunnel is an escape route for the Chief Judge if the city is under attack. As you know, it leads to the edge of the river where you can easily escape," he replied.

"Where are we?" asked Runt.

"The tunnel is directly underneath the great wall," Nephi replied.

"Where does it lead within the city?" asked Red.

"You can exit either underneath the palace, or by the wall at the edge of the city," he replied.

"Are we going to exit at the edge of the city?" asked Tulio.

"Yes, near your mother's home and my cottage," Nephi replied.

"Is this how you get in and out of the city so easily?" asked Tulio.

"Yes," Nephi replied.

"How much further do we have to travel?" asked Runt.

"Not far now," Nephi replied.

The boys walked for another five minutes before Nephi stopped. He then looked for a small scarab carved into the wall. Once located, he pushed it softly into the wall and watched as the concrete above his head slid open, revealing the bright sun overhead.

"Giddianhi's men will be searching for all of us in the city. Keep your heads down. Follow me quickly, and look at no one," he ordered.

The boys obediently followed Nephi. Stick, once again, the last to exit the tunnel, pushed the scarab stone into the wall, closing the secret opening, and then hurried to catch up with Nephi and the others. Tulio paused as they hurried past his family's home. He was thrilled at the idea of seeing his mother for the first time in over a year.

"There will be time to see her later, Tulio," called Nephi. "For your safety, follow me now."

Tulio nodded in agreement and hurried to stay close to the others.

Nephi quickly opened the door to the cottage. He walked inside and laid his friend, Samuel the Lamanite, on the bed.

"Will he be okay?" asked Bear, wondering why Samuel still had not regained consciousness.

"He will be," replied Nephi. "Tulio, bring some broth from the kettle, quickly. Stick, bring some water from the pail in the sink. Let's see if we can help the prophet regain his strength."

The boys had soon gathered the supplies Nephi needed. Then Nephi tenderly fed the prophet, until Samuel finally responded.

"Enough, enough. I can't eat anymore," Samuel insisted.

"Samuel, it is good to hear your voice, friend," said Nephi.

"So, Nephi, is it you who saved my life?" asked Samuel, trying to lift his head.

"No, Samuel, it was not me," Nephi replied.

"Then who?" he asked.

"Let me introduce you to the children who saved you. They have traveled here from another time. They were sent by the Lord to rescue you and bring you back to the city," Nephi said through a smile.

"I guess the Lord really wants me to speak to the Nephites again," Samuel said.

"Yes, Samuel, I guess he does," replied Nephi, helping him to sit up on the bed.

"What are your names?" Samuel asked, reaching his hand out to Bear.

"My name is Bear," he replied.

"That is a different name," Samuel replied. "And yours?" he asked, looking at the other boys.

"I'm Red."

"My name is Runt."

"And my name is Stick."

"Nice to meet you, boys. Thank you for saving my life. It is because of the work you've done today that thousands of people will find the true way of the Lord."

"When will you speak to the Nephites upon the wall?" asked Bear.

"How do you know of that, son?" Samuel asked.

"I've read the words the Prophet Nephi wrote about what you did to help the Nephites," he replied.

"So, the words that I speak will help them?" he asked, a little surprised.

"Yes," replied Runt. "A lot of Nephites will be helped."

"That is good to know," he replied. "Then I must stand and speak to the Nephite people ,today. Each day that passes is another day His children remain lost in darkness, without the Lord's light of truth," replied the prophet.

"Samuel, my friend, I don't know if you are strong enough to speak to the people of Zarahemla today," said Nephi, concerned for his health.

"The Lord will give me the strength to do his will," replied Samuel.

"Then you must eat some more and rest for a little while first," Nephi insisted.

"I will gladly eat more," Samuel replied. "I am really hungry."

The boys found a few figs, plums, more broth and bread for the prophet. They talked for an hour while Samuel slowly regained his strength. While he ate he told them many stories about the area.

"Nephi, can I talk to you a minute?" asked Tulio.

"Yes. What do you need?" he asked.

"I've not been this close to home in a long time. May I go and see if my mother and sister are there?" he asked.

"No," Nephi replied abruptly, surprising Tulio.

"Oh, okay, sir," Tulio replied sadly.

"Tulio, I will get them for you," he insisted, smiling. I think we will be safer if they come here to see you. Would that be alright?" he asked.

"Yes! That would be wonderful," Tulio answered, as an enormous smile spread across his face."

"I will return in a few minutes," said Nephi, as he quickly walked out the front door toward Tulio's home.

Tulio paced nervously as he waited for Nephi to return, barely hearing the stories Samuel told about his travels.

"When are you supposed to speak to the Nephites?" asked Red.

"I believe the Lord would like me to speak to them right away," he replied, standing for the first time on his own.

He was a little wobbly on his feet for the first few minutes, but quickly regained his strength.

"After Nephi returns, I will leave to speak to the people. Then I will leave this city, never to return," said Samuel.

"There is nothing left for me in this city, Samuel. May I go with you when you leave?" asked Tulio.

"Where is your family, son?" asked Samuel.

"Nephi went to get them and bring them here," Tulio replied.

"Do they want to go as well?" the prophet asked.

"I don't know, but I hope so," he replied.

"Let's decide after your family arrives," he replied cautiously.

As the front door opened, Tulio looked nervously for a familiar face. Suddenly, standing in the doorway were his mother and sister. He raced to them, threw his arms around them and cried for several minutes.

"I have to leave the city now," Tulio whispered. "Will you go with me?"

"Yes," replied his mother, squeezing her son's hand tightly. "I won't ever let you be taken from me again."

They continued to talk for several minutes, as Nephi helped Samuel plan where he should speak to the Nephite people.

Finally settling on the tallest wall in the city, the prophet announced, "The time has come for me to leave and speak to the people of this great city."

"Are we going to be able to leave with you?" asked Tulio.

"Yes. I would love to have company with me as I return to my city," said Samuel.

Nephi began to prepare for the events of the early evening. As the boys left the cottage, they were sure they would never see it again. Passing the open market, they headed for the government building and then on to the entrance of the city.

Once they reached the predetermined location, the boys watched as Samuel threw his satchel over his shoulder. It was packed with the food Nephi had given him. He hugged each of the boys and thanked them for their service. Then he turned and cautiously headed for the red stone wall of Zarahemla.

"Remember, Nephi," Samuel called, looking back over his shoulder, "get all the people baptized that are touched by my words today. Then hurry to join me."

"I will," Nephi called, waving at his friend. "Trust in the Lord, my friend. He will always be there to protect you."

"Yes, he will," replied the prophet.

Samuel paused for a moment while he looked up to the top of the wall, and then quickly started climbing the large stones toward the top of the thirty-foot wall.

"I can't believe that we're actually going to see Samuel the Lamanite talk to the people in the city of Zarahemla and call them to repentance," said Runt. "This is going to be so amazing. We get to see something that people of our day only get to read about."

"Yeah, I've read the stories and heard them in Primary and Sunday School. But, to be really honest, I never imagined them really happening," said Red. "Wow, the stories recorded in the *Book of Mormon* really are true!" exclaimed Red.

"I can't believe what the people of this great city are going to do when the prophet begins to speak," replied Stick.

"He's not going to be hurt," said Red.

"Yeah, but can you imagine throwing a rock, sword, spear or anything else at a prophet?" asked Runt. "What they're going to do today would be like you and I throwing something at our prophet back home."

"I can't even imagine," said Bear. "I could tell just by talking to Samuel that he is a prophet of God. He spoke softly, but his piercing words were the truth."

"You will not have a lot of time to stay and watch," interrupted Nephi, startling Runt. "Remember that Giddianhi and his men are still searching for you."

"You scared me, Nephi. You can't keep sneaking up on me like that," joked Runt, holding his hand to his heart.

"I'm sorry, son," Nephi replied, reaching over and tousling his hair. "I will miss you boys when you return to your homes."

"We'll miss you, too, Nephi," replied Bear.

"Look!" squealed Tulio. "There's Samuel."

Nephi and the boys watched as Samuel carefully scaled the brick wall, and made his way to the top.

Stick quickly unzipped his backpack, found his scriptures and followed along in Helaman chapter thirteen, verses five thru eight, reading to himself as Samuel began to speak.

> *"Hear me, people of Zarahemla," he started.*
> *"Behold, I, Samuel, a Lamanite, do speak the*
> *words of the Lord which he doth put into my*
> *heart; and behold he hath put it into my heart*
> *to say unto this people that the sword of justice*
> *hangeth over this people; and four hundred*
> *years pass not away save the sword of justice*
> *falleth upon this people.*

*"Yea, heavy destruction awaiteth this people,
and it surely cometh unto this people, and nothing can save this people save it be repentance
and faith on the Lord Jesus Christ, who surely
shall come into the world, and shall suffer
many things and shall be slain for his people.
"And behold, an angel of the Lord hath
declared it unto me, and he did bring glad tidings to my soul. And behold, I was sent unto
you to declare it unto you also, that ye might
have glad tidings; but behold ye would not
receive me.
"Therefore, thus saith the Lord: Because of the
hardness of the hearts of the people of the
Nephites, except they repent I will take away
my word from them, and I will withdraw my
Spirit from them, and I will suffer them no
longer, and I will turn the hearts of their
brethren against them."*

"Can you believe that we are here, listening to Samuel the Lamanite speak from the top of the wall all of the same words written in the *Book of Mormon*?" whispered Stick.

"Can you believe how the people out there are react-ing?" asked Red

"No, I can't believe that even one person would be able to hear a word that he is saying," said Bear, as he pointed to the men and women screaming obscenities at the prophet.

"I have a question," said Red, with a puzzled look on his face.

"What is it?" asked Stick.

"Well, if the prophet is free and he's speaking from the wall, as was originally written in the *Book of Mormon*, then why haven't we returned home yet?" he asked.

"I don't know. Good question," said Bear.

"Hey, we never read the scripture that the Liahona flashed earlier. Should we read it now?" asked Runt. "I have my scriptures right here."

"Yes, read the scripture for us, Runt," said Stick.

Runt nodded and quickly turned to Helaman chapter sixteen, verse one and read it to the others.

> *"'And now, it came to pass that there were many who heard the words of Samuel, the Lamanite, which he spake upon the walls of the city. And as many as believed on his word and went forth and sought for Nephi; and when they had come forth and found him they confessed unto him their sins and denied not, desiring that they might be baptized unto the Lord.'"*

"I think the scripture is telling us that we needed to save the Prophet Samuel so that many of the people could go to Nephi and be baptized," said Stick.

"I agree," said Bear.

"Bear, was that all you saw on the Liahona?" asked Runt.

"No, there were several symbols. But I didn't know

what they were," he replied.

"I wonder if there is also something else that we are supposed to do?" asked Red.

"What? What else is there to do?" asked Bear.

"Boys," interrupted Nephi. "We're in danger. We must leave right now."

"Why? What's the matter?" asked Red. "I wanted to listen to the rest of Samuel's speech."

"There isn't time. The Lord will keep Samuel safe. However, we must leave immediately. Now, follow me," Nephi ordered.

After finding a suitable hiding place, Nephi said, "I'm afraid that it is time for you boys to return home."

"We can't," said Stick, wrinkling his forehead. "Until we fix all that we were sent here to do, the Liahona will not take us back to our time."

"What have you not done?" asked Nephi, as he crouched in the tall trees with the rest of the boys.

"We don't know," answered Bear.

"Then I must return you to the safety of the cottage, before you are discovered," Nephi replied.

"This is where we must say goodbye," said Tulio.

"What do you mean?" asked Runt. "Why aren't you coming with us?"

"I am leaving the city with Samuel today, as soon as he is finished speaking, remember?" Tulio responded.

"Thanks for everything that you did for us," said Stick. "We never could have done any of this without your help."

Chapter Twenty-One

Tulio threw his arms around the boys and hugged them. He was sad he would not see them again. Finally, he managed to say, "Goodbye."

"We will never forget you, Tulio," whimpered Red, as he patted his new friend on the back. "Thank you for everything you've done for us."

"Thank you for everything you've done for me. My family would never have been free of Giddianhi's rule without your help," Tulio replied softly, choking back the tears.

He looked up and smiled, then turned and disappeared with his family into the thick jungle of trees.

"It is time to go," said Nephi. "I must meet my friend, Morihan, before I return you to the cottage."

Nephi scurried through the trees, being careful to stay hidden from Giddianhi's soldiers.

"Nephi, wait!" called Stick.

"There is no time," he called over his shoulder. "I'm going to be late."

"No, wait!" insisted Runt. "We've got to talk to you. It's very important."

"Later," Nephi answered. "I must hurry."

"No, now! Or I'm not taking one more step," said Bear.

"What, boys?" asked Nephi, exasperated by their actions. He quickly walked back toward them and again asked, "What?"

"We need to talk to you about Morihan," Stick replied.

"Well, you'll have to talk to me while I walk. I do not want to be late for my meeting with Morihan. He's waiting for me right now in the market." replied Nephi, walking in that direction. "Now, what do you need to tell me boys?"

"Nephi, Morihan is one of Giddianhi's men," Stick said nervously.

"No, he's not," replied Nephi, dismissing the statement as completely absurd.

"Nephi, he was one of the men who chased us the first night that we came to your city," said Runt.

"And he was the man that found where I was hiding, and took me to Giddianhi," added Bear.

"He was also in Gadianton's secret tunnels when we were trying to save Bear and Samuel," added Red.

"I don't believe it!" Nephi replied.

"But, it's true, Nephi," Stick insisted.

"How? When?" Nephi mumbled, under his breath. "He has been my trusted friend for years."

"We heard him talking with Giddianhi's men in the tunnels. He said that he had you under surveillance, and that once the prophet was killed, you would be next," said Stick.

"We didn't want to say anything, but we don't want you to get hurt either," added Bear.

"I appreciate that, boys," replied Nephi softly as they arrived at the edge of the market.

Nephi looked out at his childhood friend, innocently waiting for him in the crowded market.

"Is there anything we can do?" asked Runt.

"Yes, stay hidden," he replied. "I don't want Giddianhi's men to find you."

"Me, neither," said Red. "So, where should we hide? We can't stay in the jungle, they will find us here eventually."

"You are right," replied Nephi. "We should return to the cot...," he started. He sat quietly for several minutes before he finally replied, "I told him about you boys, and he knows about my cottage. We cannot return there now. We will have to find another safe place."

"We could hide up in the barn," suggested Red.

"No, Captain Gilead will tear it apart looking for Tulio," Nephi replied. He looked at Morihan, pacing back and forth, and asked, "Are you sure, boys?"

"Sure of what?" asked Stick.

"Sure that my good friend, Morihan, has betrayed

me?" Nephi asked, as a tear trickled down his face.

Stick looked down at the ground. Trying not to tear up, he was sad that he had to be the one to tell Nephi about Morihan. He looked up and pulled the leaves from the palm tree aside, just enough to get a good look at Morihan.

Stick studied the expression on Morihan's face and replied, "I am positive, Nephi. I personally saw him in the waterway the night we arrived. I saw and heard his voice in the tunnels underneath the city. And I also saw him talking to Giddianhi. I'm so sorry."

Nephi watched his friend for several minutes. He finally looked away and wiped the tears from his eyes. He sighed and said, "Well, then it is time to leave this city."

"You can't leave Zarahemla," Bear protested.

"If what you boys are telling me is true, then I must leave the city of Zarahemla immediately," replied Nephi.

"But you can't," insisted Runt.

"Why? If my life is in danger, then I must leave," replied Nephi. "I have much more work that I need to do for the Lord."

"That's right. That is why you cannot leave," said Bear.

"I do not understand," said Nephi. "You tell me my friend is not a friend. You tell me my life is in danger. But then you tell me that I cannot leave the city, where men seek to take away my life? asked Nephi. "I would never have believed that Morihan would do anything to betray me. I now understand how secret information about where and when I entered the city was being divulged."

"Nephi," started Stick, as he took a big breath,

"because of the speech that Samuel gives today, more than eight thousand Nephites repent and come to you to be baptized."

"Because of the speech he now gives on the wall?" questioned Nephi.

"Yes," replied Stick.

"I think that is why the Lord had the Liahona bring us to your time," said Bear.

"We needed to save the prophet, so that he could call the people to repentance," added Red.

"Many people will have a change of heart today. They will seek the Lord's mercy through repentance. They will then come to you to be baptized, in hopes that they can someday return to live with our Father in Heaven," said Runt.

"Then you came not only to save the Prophet Samuel, but also to save me," said Nephi, smiling at the boys.

"Nephi, look!" Bear called frantically.

"What, son?" asked Nephi.

He followed Bear's finger, which was pointing toward the market. As Nephi looked, he saw Morihan standing with Ethem, Shiz, Lib and Giddianhi. Giddianhi seemed to be doing all the talking. The boys and Nephi watched as Morihan shrugged his shoulder and pointed to the sun. They were sure he was telling Giddianhi that Nephi was late.

They watched for nearly five minutes, bewildered by the actions of Giddianhi. Morihan startled Nephi when he drew his sword, waving it in the air wildly. His actions were followed by the other soldiers. Giddianhi was the last to draw his sword. The boys watched as he made several announcements to the crowd.

"Can you hear anything he's saying?" asked Bear.

"I heard him yell your name, Nephi," said Runt.

"So did I, boys," replied Nephi. "I'm convinced that the Lord truly sent you to save me."

"Whatever the reason," Bear began, "I'm glad to have met you."

Nephi nodded, smiled and said, "It is time for us to find a new place to hide."

"Do you know of any other safe places?" asked Red.

"Yes," replied Nephi. "I have another small cottage, one that no one knows of—not even Morihan. We will go there."

"Where is it?" asked Stick.

"It is on the east edge of the city, near the lake," he replied.

"I bet that is where you will baptize all of the Nephite people," Stick said excitedly.

"That could very well be," Nephi replied. He turned from the market and started to walk deeper and deeper into the jungle of Zarahemla.

The boys followed Nephi quietly for a long time. When they finally arrived at Nephi's secret cottage, they had to cut through the vines that had overgrown the front door.

"You should be safe here, Nephi," said Runt. "No one will be able to find you with all the plants and vines around the house."

"I think we will all be safe here," replied Nephi. "Until it is time for you to return home."

They walked inside where Nephi started a fire and placed a blanket on the floor. Are you boys as hungry as I am?" he asked.

"Hungrier, I think," replied Runt, holding his stomach.

"Good. Then I will gather some food, and we will have something to eat," he replied.

Suddenly, a bright light shined through the top of Bear's backpack, filling Nephi's home with warmth. Unsure what was happening, Bear stood up and pulled his backpack off his shoulders.

"What did you do, Bear?" asked Red.

"I didn't do anything!" he replied defensively

"It looks to me like your journey is through," said Nephi. "A light that shines that bright can only mean one thing."

"What is that, Nephi?" asked Stick, as he looked worriedly at the light shining from his backpack.

"That is the Light of Christ, boys. He is happy with what you have done here," replied Nephi.

"I'm going to miss you, Nephi," said Bear, as he wrapped his arms tightly around Nephi's waist.

"I'm going to miss you boys, too," replied Nephi, as his voice crack slightly. "I hope that someday I will get to see you again," said Nephi.

"Me, too," replied Runt. "I wish that we could choose where the Liahona takes us next time."

"Well, if the Lord ever desires you to visit me again, I will look forward to that day," said Nephi, as he patted Stick on the back. "The people in your time are very lucky to have the strength of your testimonies."

"Thank you," said Runt.

"The light is flashing, boys," said Nephi. "It is time for you to go."

Bear quickly unzipped the front pocket of his backpack, revealing the beautifully ornate Liahona.

"Stick, Nephi is right. The panel on the Liahona is flashing!" exclaimed Bear.

"What numbers are flashing this time?" asked Stick. "Are we going home?"

"No numbers are flashing—just a solid white panel," Bear replied.

"Nephi, I think you're right. It's time for us to go!" hollered Red. He grabbed his backpack and moved closer to Bear. "Stay back, Nephi! We don't want you to end up stuck in the future."

Nephi smiled and watched as the Liahona flashed the brightest light he had ever seen. And then, before his very eyes, Stick, Bear, Red and Runt disappeared.

The panel and light suddenly went dark. The team-mates tried to look around, but their surroundings were pitch black. With the unexpected bright flash of light, their eyes needed a minute to adjust.

"Are we home?" asked Stick.

"I don't think we've even moved yet," replied Red. "Nephi, are you here?" he called.

The boys listened for a response, but all they could hear was silence.

"Maybe we are home," Bear said optimistically.

"I don't remember moving before we landed in the water," replied Runt. "So, we could be home."

"Well, that's true. Should I try to move?" asked Red.

"You could try, but be careful. I don't want anyone to get hurt," answered Stick. "And I can't see a thing."

"This doesn't feel right to me," said Bear. "I think maybe we're on another mission. We better be careful."

"Hero and those guys came back after their mission. Why shouldn't we?" asked Stick. "I hope we've gone home. I'm starving! I need some real food."

"I can't see anything," complained Red, frustrated at the lack of light. "I think I could see better in the tunnels."

"Stick, don't you have a flashlight or something?" asked Bear.

"No, Runt dropped mine in the snake pit, remember?" he replied.

"What about the glow stick? Is it still working, Red?" asked Runt.

"They only work for twelve hours," he replied. "And it was weak the last time we used it. I can't imagine that it still has any light left."

"What about you, Bear? Do you have a flashlight in your backpack?" asked Stick.

"I don't have a flashlight, but I think I have a light for when I use my Gameboy in the dark. Would that give enough light?"

"Yeah, that should work," replied Red. "Where is it?"

"Somewhere in my backpack," Bear replied.

"Well, try to find it," urged Stick. "I keep trying to feel with my foot for somewhere that I can take a step, but without any light, I can't find anything."

"Okay, hold on. I'm sure it's here somewhere," replied Bear, as he rummaged quickly through his pack, searching for the light.

Several anxious seconds passed before Red impatiently asked, "Bear, come on already. Did you find the light yet?"

"I'm working on it, Red," he snapped.

Finally finding the light, he pointed it toward what he hoped was the ground and turned it on.

Several moments later, as their eyes adjusted, Runt squealed, "I know where we are."

"Me, too," added Red excitedly.

"Well, I don't," said Bear. "Where are we?"

"I should have known that the treasure would bring

us back inside the tree, just like it did when Hero came home," reasoned Stick. "This is where we found the Liahona."

"What are you talking about?" asked Bear, obviously confused.

"We must be back home," said Runt. "I recognize the smell of the air."

"Come on, guys. Let's get out of here and go find the rest of the Team," insisted Red. He turned carefully and climbed down the knotted and gnarled edges inside the tree.

"Get out of where?" questioned Bear. "Where are we?"

"Just follow me, Bear," replied Red.

Everyone followed Red to the bottom of the tree, and then exited through the small opening into the bright light outside.

"I can't wait to show everyone the clothes Tulio gave us to wear," said Runt.

"I can't wait to change out of these clothes," said Stick, smiling. "And take a shower with soap and shampoo."

"Well, I can't wait to tell the Team everything we saw and did," replied Bear.

"Remember, Bear, you've got to be careful who you talk to about the Liahona and the adventure we've just gone on," Stick said sternly. "We could end up in a lot of trouble if anyone ever found out."

"Not to mention danger," said Red.

"Yeah, I don't want to end up like Mr. Jensen's grandfather," added Runt. "Missing or Dead."

"I never thought about it until now," said Stick, "but I wonder if Mr. Jensen's grandfather didn't solve the mystery fast enough, so he had to stay in whatever land he was sent to?"

"I guess that's possible," reasoned Runt.

"I wonder if he was taken somewhere and decided he liked it, so he just stayed," said Bear. "I can see that."

"Forever in the past?" asked Red. "No way!"

"I think it might be cool," replied Bear.

"Look, the ladder is down. The Team must be up in the Treehouse waiting for us," said Red.

"Let's go see if we can find them," called Runt, as he started to climb the ladder.

"Yeah, we better find them before anyone finds us," said Stick.

"We've got to find the team and have them tell us everything that's happened. That way we won't say or do something that we shouldn't," added Runt.

"I wonder what time it is," said Red.

"I wonder what day it is," said Bear.

"I'm just glad to be home," said Stick. "No matter what time or day it is."

"I agree," added Bear. "I can't wait to see everyone and tell them all about our adventure."

"Even though Hero is going to be mad at us?" asked Red, as he climbed up the ladder.

"I hadn't thought about that," replied Bear.

"He will probably be glad that we are back safe, and then he's going to be a little mad," replied Runt. "We did sneak up here and mess around with the Liahona after he told us not to."

"I'm sure Hero will be fine," replied Red. "Especially since we're home safe."

Chapter Twenty-Two

"We're home! Everybody, we're home!" yelled Bear excitedly. "We figured out the problem, and we made it home."

"Home from where?" asked Mrs. M, startling Bear.

"I didn't expect to see you up in the Treehouse, Auntie," replied Bear. He looked around frantically for any sign of Hero and Bubba. "Where is everybody?"

"Well Bear, why don't you tell me?" insisted Mrs. M, "I thought for some silly reason that the entire Team was off hunting for treasure—together!"

"Did you tell everybody we're back from our adventure into another land, Bear?" interrupted Stick, as he threw open the door and rushed inside. "I can't wait to tell you guys all about it."

"I was just talking to Hero and Bubba's mom," replied Bear, making a face at Stick.

"So, boys, come in and tell me where you've been," Mrs. M. requested suspiciously. "I can't wait to hear about your adventure into another land."

"Hi, Mrs. M. How are you?" asked Red, as he and Runt climbed inside the Treehouse.

"Hi, boys. Where is the rest of the Team?" asked Mrs. M.

"I'm not sure," replied Runt. "I had to run home for a little while."

Mrs. M. nodded her head and squinted her eyes tightly, sure the boys were not telling her the truth. She sat silently studying their faces, watching them squirm.

Stick couldn't stand the silence anymore and said, "Mrs. M., I've never seen you up in the Treehouse before. Did you need something?"

"Well, Stick, weren't you going to find the walkie-talkie that belonged in the house and return it to me yesterday?" she asked. "Oddly enough, I haven't seen you since then."

"I sure was," he answered. "I completely forgot. I'm so sorry. I have your walkie-talkie right here in my backpack. Let me get it for you right now."

Mrs. M. watched silently, skeptical of the four boys. Stick unzipped the backpack and fumbled nervously through its contents. Several tense moments passed as Stick searched.

He finally pulled his hand from the backpack and squealed, "I found it!"

Smiling, he carried the walkie-talkie over and placed it on the table.

"Sorry for the delay! I really did just forget to bring it back to you," Stick added quietly, avoiding eye contact.

"Yesterday, I was okay without having the walkie-talkie. But I have not been able to get a hold of the boys today. I sure wish the four of you would tell me what's going on," said Mrs. M. "Is Hero in some kind of trouble?"

"I promise, Auntie, I don't know where they are right now. I decided to help Stick get some stuff done today. I told Hero and Bubba that we would meet them back at the Treehouse as soon as we could," explained Bear.

"Can you tell me if whatever they're doing has something to do with Moroni's Treasure Map?" asked Mrs. M. "Or are they doing something that could get them in trouble?"

"Well, you know that we've been trying really hard to solve the clues on the map," replied Red. "I don't think Hero would do anything on purpose to get into trouble."

"So, does that mean he's working on solving the map, or is he doing something else?" she pressed.

"Last I saw him, he was working on stuff that had to do with Moroni's Map," replied Stick.

"Is the rest of the team with him?" Mrs. M. quizzed. She leaned forward in her chair, placed her hands on her knees, squinted her eyes tightly and waited for a response.

"I...I think so," stammered Runt. "But I'm really not sure."

"Okay, boys, I won't make you lie to me anymore. If you don't want to tell me what is really going on, I won't make you," Mrs. M. said. She took a deep breath and shaking her head she let it out with a sigh. "But I wish you would trust me enough to let me know what is happening. Where is that walkie-talkie, Stick?" asked Mrs. M.

"Right there, on the table," he replied, pointing.

"Are the batteries working?" she asked, as she turned the black knob to the ON position.

"They're working, but they don't have a lot of power left," added Stick. "I've tried to call Hero several times in the last few hours, but I haven't been able to reach him."

"Hero's batteries might be dead, too," suggested Runt.

"Either that, or his walkie-talkie could be just out of range," said Red.

"That's true. It could be out of range," agreed Stick, suddenly noticing the clothes they were wearing.

"I will check the batteries when I get downstairs," Mrs. M replied, as she walked to the door. "Oh, and one more thing—after you boys get changed into twenty-first century clothes, all of you, including Hero, Bubba and Squeaks, can come down and tell me the truth about what has been going on around here."

"Oh, these clothes?" asked Stick, looking down at the knee-length skirt he was wearing. "We thought it would be fun to dress up like characters from the *Book of Mormon* while we searched for clues. You know, we think we're gonna find Moroni's Treasure any time now. And what if it's protected by a soldier or something?"

"Is that your story too, Bear?" Mrs. M. asked, looking closely at the reaction on his face.

"Yes, don't you think we look good?" Bear asked, with a cheesy grin on his face.

"Look good? I'm not sure I'd go that far. But what I am impressed with is the authentic red dirt and the horrible smell of boys who have not showered or used deodorant for a few days. How did you truthfully do that overnight?" Mom asked. She walked out the Treehouse door, closing it firmly behind her.

"Oh, man, Stick. She knows. We are gonna be in so much trouble," whined Bear. "And if she tells my mom, I'm gonna be in even more trouble."

"She doesn't know what's going on. She only knows that something doesn't seem right. How could she know anything about the Liahona?" asked Stick. "No one but Cheri even knows that we have it."

"Do you think Cheri called her?" asked Runt.

"No, Cheri wouldn't tell anyone unless one of us was hurt or something was seriously wrong," said Red.

"I can't believe that she was up here searching for the walkie-talkie," said Stick. "I didn't think that she would ever come up here—especially since she is afraid of heights."

"She must be really worried about the Team," added Runt.

"Maybe she has a sixth sense, and she can tell that something is going on," suggested Red, as he started changing his clothes.

"I don't know about a sixth sense, but maybe a mother's intuition—especially where Hero and Bubba are concerned," said Red. "My mom seems to know when something's not right with me."

"I wonder where everybody is," said Bear. "I was excited to tell them about our adventure."

"We don't have any way to find out, because Hero's mom has the walkie-talkie now," said Stick.

"Bring in the telescope. Let's look and see if she set it on the charger," suggested Bear. "If she did, maybe we can borrow it for a minute."

Runt hurried out to the balcony of the Treehouse and grabbed the telescope. He pointed the lens directly toward the kitchen window, and looked to see if the walkie-talkie was visible.

"I can see it. She just set it on the charger!" he yelled excitedly.

"I'm gonna go and see if I can get it without her seeing," said Bear.

He climbed down the ladder and headed toward the sliding glass door. Runt watched as Bear sneaked behind the bushes. He poked his head from behind them only long enough to find his next hiding spot. As he finally reached the door, he peered inside for any sign of his aunt. Not seeing her anywhere, he opened the door and headed straight for the walkie-talkie.

Suddenly, Runt caught a glimpse of Hero's mom hiding in the kitchen. He tried to warn Bear, but it was too late. She waited for Bear to reach for the walkie-talkie before she grabbed his hand.

"Aaaaaaaaahhhhhhhhhhhhhh!" screamed Bear.

"What are you doing, Bear?" she demanded, holding on to his arm.

"You scared me!" he screamed, still shaking. "I've had a rough few days."

"Well, if you would tell me why, then maybe I could help you," Hero's mom replied. "Now tell me, what are you doing?"

"I was gonna borrow the walkie-talkie just for a second. We wanted to see if we could get a hold of Hero," Bear replied, trying to pull his arm free.

"Alright, now I really want to know what is going on around here," she said.

"Hey, Bear. What's going on, bud," said Hero, as he strolled casually into the kitchen.

"Hey, Hero. It's good to see you," Bear replied.

"Hero, where have you been, and why haven't you been checking in on the walkie-talkie?" Mom asked, nearly shouting.

"I'm sorry, Mom. The batteries went dead, and we didn't have any extras. Did you need me?" Hero asked.

"Where have you been?" she demanded.

"Out looking for Moroni's Treasure. We told you where we were going before we left," Hero answered defensively.

"That was this morning at ten o'clock! It is now seven in the evening. That's a long time to be gone," said Mom. "That's it, Hero! Get everybody up to the Treehouse. We are having a talk, right now!"

Mom led the way, with Hero, Bubba, Bean, Butch,

Tater, KP, Bear and Squeaks following closely behind.

"Hey, Stick everybody's coming," announced Runt. "Including Hero's mom."

"What? Hero's mom is coming back up?" he asked, moving quickly to look over the balcony.

As she reached the top, Mrs. M. stomped inside the Treehouse. She motioned for Hero to close the door, and said, "All right, Team, either someone tells me exactly what is going on around here, or the Treehouse is closed for the rest of the summer. And Hero, Bubba and Squeaks will be grounded—forever!"

"Mom? What are you talking about?" asked Bubba.

"Don't even go there with me, son. I know you've found something, and I want to know what it is. And I mean right now!" she demanded.

"Mom, really, I don't...," started Squeaks.

"Don't lie for them, Squeaks. You're just gonna get yourself into more trouble," Mom interrupted.

"I think our fun is up," said Hero sadly. "We wanted to tell you, Mom, but we were afraid that you wouldn't let us use it."

"Use what, Hero? What are you talking about?" asked Mom, still scowling.

"Mom, would you get mad if I told you a secret?" asked Squeaks.

"Why would I get mad? Have you done something wrong?" Mom asked.

"No! I haven't done anything wrong!" she replied defensively.

"If you haven't done anything wrong, then what are

you afraid of, Team?" Mom asked, confused by their behavior.

Bubba took a deep breath, looked around at everyone and said, "You know we have to show her, right?"

"Where is it, Stick?" asked Tater.

"It's in your backpack. The one I just brought back with me," he replied. "But you better be careful."

Mom watched quietly as Tater walked to the backpack. He unzipped the main pocket and pulled out the beautiful Liahona. As he started to walk toward Hero's mom, he said, "We actually found the treasure a few days ago."

"What is it?" she asked, puzzled by the object he held.

"This is the Liahona. It has the power to take people back in time, to places in the *Book of Mormon*. The people are sent on small missions by the Lord, and must fix something that has gone wrong," Tater explained.

"What in the world?" Mom said to herself. She paused for a moment and then blurted out, "Have you used it to go somewhere already?"

"Well, we don't really get to chose when we go. The Lord decides for us," Hero answered.

"That is not what I asked, Hero. Have you used it yet?" she asked insistently.

"Yeah, Bubba and I have," he replied slowly, dreading her reaction.

"Oh, my! Are you serious? You and your brother have traveled somewhere in *Book of Mormon* times?" she asked.

"Yes, Mom," Bubba replied.

"Where? When?"

"Back to the time of Captain Moroni and Lehi," Bubba replied.

"You didn't fight in a battle, did you?" she asked nervously.

"No, but we did see a battle," said Bean, as she walked closer to Mrs. M.

"You went, too?" she asked, obviously surprised. "Who else?"

"Hero, Bubba, KP and I went on the first adventure," Bean replied.

"Has there been more than one adventure already?" asked Mrs. M.

"Yeah. Stick, Red, Runt and I just got back a few minutes ago," said Bear.

"You've got to be kidding!" she replied in disbelief. "Bear, your Mom would kill me if she knew I let you travel back in time. Where did you travel to?"

"We went to the time of Samuel the Lamanite," Bear excitedly replied. "We got to save him. It was scary, but great."

"Let me see this thing," she insisted, as she held out her hand. "Is there anyone who has not gone, besides me?" Mrs. M. asked, looking closely at every detail.

"I haven't gone," squealed Squeaks.

"Neither have I," added Butch.

"Me either, Mrs. M," said Tater.

"You aren't making this entire thing up are you?" she asked, looking right at Hero.

"Nope," Hero answered.

"How did you do all of this without me knowing?" questioned Mom.

"You've been busy, Mom," replied Squeaks.

"Boy, I guess I need to pay more attention," Mom replied.

"Are you mad, Mrs. M?" asked Red.

"No, I'm not mad. This is amazing!" she replied. "I am a little concerned however, that my kids were time traveling, and they didn't even tell me."

"I couldn't tell you, Mom," insisted Bubba. "The Liahona flashes three times, and then, whoever is closest to it, gets taken on the next adventure—whether they planned on going or not."

"So, the flash of light I saw the other day was the four of you traveling in time?" asked Mom. "And is that why you were wearing those clothes earlier, boys?"

"Yep," replied Stick, through a nervous smile. "We just got back."

"So, exactly what flashes?" asked Mom.

"The panel on the front flashes a number, which we've learned, is the year you will travel to," Hero replied. "Then suddenly you're gone."

"Hey, we better get the Liahona back in its box before it starts to flash again," suggested Bubba, as turned to get the case for his Mom.

"Hero, what kind of flashing?" asked Mom nervously. "Flashing like this?"

"Oh, please no!" screamed Hero.

He lunged toward her, trying to take the Liahona.

But, before Hero was able to take even one step, a bright light flashed, filling the room. Hero held up his hand to shield his eyes. When he could finally see again, Mom, Squeaks, Tater and Butch had vanished.

"No, no, no, no, no! What am I going to tell Dad?" screamed Hero. "It's not like I can tell him that Mom is at a sleep-over!"

"Hero, do you think Mom can handle this?" asked Bubba in a teary voice.

"I don't know, Bubba. I sure hope so," Hero replied, as he dropped his head into his hands and sank to his knees.

❋

The Titan's have another date with destiny...Where will they end up next?

About the Author

Although born in Provo, Utah, Tina spent most of her life in San Diego, California. Her writing is strongly influenced by her hometown experiences and her large family whose flair for story telling never ends.

As a direct descendant of Heber C. Kimball and Orson Pratt, the stories told to her by her parents about them encouraged a fascination with the Book of Mormon, Church history, and the adventures of the early saints.

Tina Storrs Monson currently lives in Draper Utah, a suburb of Salt Lake City. She attended Brigham Young University where she met her husband, Kreg. They have been married for seventeen years and have four children.